S0-AAB-730

"The Golden Nugget is a permanent fixture here in Thunder Canyon. I'm not."

At Mia's words, Marshall's spoon paused in midair as he frowned. "You're not leaving soon, are you?"

His finger slid beneath her chin and lifted her face up to his. The serious look she saw on his handsomely carved features sent her heart into a heavy rapid thud.

"We're just getting to know each other, Mia. I'd really like you to stay longer."

His voice tugged at her every feminine particle. "I—uh—I'll think about it."

Suddenly his head was bending toward hers, and the whisper that passed his lips skittered down her spine.

"Maybe you should think about this."

Longing held her motionless as his lips descended onto hers....

Dear Reader,

I was thrilled when asked to do a MONTANA MAVERICKS book, and when I learned the theme—striking it rich—I knew it was a subject that would touch everyone. After all, haven't we all wondered what it would be like to hit the lottery or fall into sudden fortune? Ahh, the things we could do with all that money. Shopping till we dropped. Traveling around the world. Indulging ourselves with anything and everything we've ever wanted. Sounds good, huh? Sounds like all our problems would be solved. Or so my heroine thinks.

After scratching her way through years of poverty, Mia believes money is all she needs to fix the troubles in her life. But when a fortune suddenly befalls her, she slowly and painfully begins to see that being rich in money is not nearly as great as being rich in love.

I hope you enjoy reading how Mia finds the real treasures in her life!

God bless you with life's true riches,

Stella Bagwell

STELLA BAGWELL

PAGING DR. RIGHT

SPECIAL EDITION

Published by Silhouette Books

America's Publisher of Contemporary Romance

If you purchased this book without a cover you should be aware
that this book is stolen property. It was reported as "unsold and
destroyed" to the publisher, and neither the author nor the
publisher has received any payment for this "stripped book."

Special thanks and acknowledgment are given
to Stella Bagwell for her contribution to
the MONTANA MAVERICKS:
STRIKING IT RICH miniseries.

SILHOUETTE BOOKS

ISBN-13: 978-0-373-28091-9
ISBN-10:   0-373-28091-2

PAGING DR. RIGHT

Copyright © 2007 by Harlequin Books S.A.

All rights reserved. Except for use in any review, the reproduction
or utilization of this work in whole or in part in any form by any
electronic, mechanical or other means, now known or hereafter
invented, including xerography, photocopying and recording, or in
any information storage or retrieval system, is forbidden without
the written permission of the editorial office, Silhouette Books,
233 Broadway, New York, NY 10279 U.S.A.

This is a work of fiction. Names, characters, places and incidents are
either the product of the author's imagination or are used fictitiously, and
any resemblance to actual persons, living or dead, business establishments,
events or locales is entirely coincidental.

This edition published by arrangement with Harlequin Books S.A.

® and TM are trademarks of Harlequin Books S.A., used under license.
Trademarks indicated with ® are registered in the United States Patent
and Trademark Office, the Canadian Trade Marks Office and in other
countries.

Visit Silhouette Books at www.eHarlequin.com

Printed in U.S.A.

Books by Stella Bagwell

Silhouette Special Edition

Found: One Runaway Bride #1049
*_Penny Parker's Pregnant!_ #1258
White Dove's Promise #1478
†*Should Have Been Her Child* #1570
†*His Defender* #1582
†*Her Texas Ranger* #1622
†*A Baby on the Ranch* #1648
In a Texas Minute #1677
†*Redwing's Lady* #1695
†*From Here to Texas* #1700
†*Taming a Dark Horse* #1709
†*A South Texas Christmas* #1789
†*The Rancher's Request* #1802
†*The Best Catch in Texas* #1814
†*Having the Cowboy's Baby* #1828
***Paging Dr. Right* #1843

Silhouette Books

The Fortunes of Texas
    The Heiress and the Sheriff

Maitland Maternity
    Just for Christmas

A Bouquet of Babies
    *"Baby on Her Doorstep"

Midnight Clear
    *"Twins under the Tree"

Going to the Chapel
    "The Bride's Big Adventure"

*Twins on the Doorstep
†Men of the West
**Montana Mavericks: Striking It Rich

STELLA BAGWELL

sold her first novel to Silhouette Books in November 1985. She still loves her job and says she isn't completely content unless she's writing. She and her husband live in Seadrift, Texas, a sleepy little fishing town located on the coastal bend, where the water, the tropical climate and the seabirds make it a lovely place to let her imagination soar and to put the stories in her head down on paper.

She and her husband have one son, Jason, who lives and teaches high school math in nearby Port Lavaca.

To my family—the real golden nuggets in my life.

Chapter One

Was this his lucky day or what?

Using the back of his arm, Marshall Cates wiped the sweat streaming into his eyes and peered a second time at the woman sitting on a boulder some twenty feet below. From his precarious position on the rock ledge, the only view he had was of a portion of her back, the long fall of her raven-black hair and her nipped-in waist; but those tempting glimpses were enough to tell him it was *the heiress*.

For the past three weeks every male employee at Thunder Canyon Resort had been talking and fantasizing about the mystery guest. So far Marshall had only gazed at her from afar and wondered what a beautiful young woman with money to burn was doing here alone in Thunder Canyon. True, the small western Montana town was growing in leaps and bounds and Thunder Canyon Resort, where he worked as staff doctor, was garnering a reputation for fine hospitality surrounded by scenic splendor. The clientele was becoming ritzy, flying in from all corners of the nation. Still, Marshall couldn't help but figure a woman with her apparent class would rather be vacationing on the French Riviera than in the middle of a cowman's paradise. The fact that she appeared to be here without an escort intrigued him even more.

This morning, Marshall had risen early, wondering what to do with his off-duty time. With his brothers and his buddies all tied up with other interests, he'd eventually decided to do something he loved, climbing, and had headed up one of the mountains near the resort. When he'd set out on this trek, he'd never dreamed that the chance to meet Ms. Heiress would present itself on the edge of a rocky bluff. Since he'd only ever spotted her lounging around the lodge, he hadn't figured her for a nature girl.

Quickly, he rappelled the last few feet of the layered rock until his boots hit solid ground. Once there, he gathered up his climbing equipment and left his ropes, rings and anchors in a neat pile with his backpack.

As Marshall walked over to the woman he noticed she was sitting near an opening in the trees, looking out toward the endless valley that swept away from the mountain range. The view was majestic, especially to someone who'd never seen the landscape before. But this woman didn't appear to be enjoying the scenery; she was deep in thought. So much so that she was completely unaware of his presence.

Fearing his approach might scare her so badly she'd fall from the boulder, he stopped ten feet from her and called out.

"Hello there."

The moment she heard his voice, her head whipped around and her palms flattened against the rock in preparation to push herself to her feet. Surprise was etched upon her parted lips and wide eyes, telling him she'd definitely believed herself to be totally alone on this particular piece of mountain. She was dressed in khaki shorts that struck her mid-thigh, a pale pink T-shirt that hugged her breasts and sturdy brown hiking boots. Her hair hung like shiny satin against her shoulders.

An enchanting princess sitting on her throne, he thought, as he felt every male particle in him begin to buzz with excitement.

"Sorry if I scared you," Marshall went on before she could gather herself enough to speak. "I saw you sitting here and thought I'd say hello."

Slowly, warily, she eased her bottom back on the boulder and her dark eyes carefully monitored his movements as he came to stand a few feet beside her. Marshall wondered if he really looked that sinister. It was an odd thought for a doctor who'd taken an oath to save lives, not harm them. But Ms. Heiress didn't know him and he supposed she was wise not to trust a strange man out in the wilderness.

Finally, she returned his greeting with a faint nod of her regal head. "Hello."

Spoken quietly, that one word was clear and without a hint of accent, giving little clue as to where she might live. However, it did tell Marshall that she'd not traveled up to Thunder Canyon from a Southern state.

Giving her the sort of smile he reserved for skittish female patients, he asked, "Enjoying the warm weather?"

Actually, it had been downright hot. Not an unusual occurrence for August, but it would take a native like himself to know the nuances of Thunder Canyon climate and right at this moment he wasn't ready to let this beautiful sophisticate know he was a born-and-bred local. She might just snub her straight little nose at him and walk off, and he was too curious about the woman to take that chance.

"Very much," she quietly replied.

Marshall took two steps forward, all the while feeling her dark eyes gliding over him, weighing him as though she were trying to decide if he was worthy of conversation. The idea irked Marshall just a bit. Especially since he was accustomed to women smiling warmly at him, not studying him like a bug on a leaf.

"The view is beautiful from here," she suddenly went on. "The sky seems to go on forever and I was thinking about hanging around to see the sunset this evening, but I suppose being caught out here in the dark wouldn't be wise."

At least the woman had a little common sense to go with all that beauty, he thought, as his gaze covertly slid down a pair of long shapely legs. Her skin was slightly kissed by the sun and the warm gleam told him it would be butter smooth beneath his hand.

Trying not to dwell on that pleasant thought, he shook his head. "No. I wouldn't recommend being here on the mountains after dark. Black bears and mountain lions are spotted in this area from time to time. You wouldn't want to meet up with any of those."

Glancing at the forest surrounding them, she said, "I've noticed the warnings signs on the hiking trails and read the information posted in the lodge." She lifted one hand and shook a bracelet adorned with sleigh bells. "Just to be safe I wore a bear bracelet. I was told the sound would scare the creatures away."

"So they say." He didn't go on to tell her that as a teenager he'd had his own run-in with a black bear and that the sow had refused to back down until his brother had shot a round from his hunting rifle over the angry animal's head. Scaring the woman would hardly be the way to entice her into further conversation.

To Marshall's surprise, she suddenly climbed down from the rock and stood within an arm's length from him. The short distance was enough to give him a clear view of her face. High rounded cheekbones, a dainty dimpled chin and full lips were perfectly sculpted out of creamy skin. Her eyes, which appeared dark from a distance, were actually a blend of earthy green and brown, outlined by a thick fringe of jet-black lashes. Above them, delicate brows of the same color arched into a smooth, wide forehead. At the moment, the corners of her pink lips were curved faintly upward and Marshall could hardly tear his gaze away.

"You've been mountain climbing?" she asked, her gaze sweeping past him to the mound of equipment he'd left beneath the rocky bluff.

"Since this morning," he answered. "I didn't make it all the way to the top, but far enough for a good workout."

Her gaze pulled back to him and he could feel it sliding over his sweaty face and down to the damp patch in the middle of his black T-shirt. Normally when a woman looked at him, Marshall didn't give it a second thought. But Ms. Heiress was studying him in a way that left him close to blushing. Something he hadn't done since his sophomore year in high school.

"I hiked up this far, but when I ran into the rock bluff I realized this would be as far as I could go," she said a bit wistfully. "Is this something you do often?"

His smile crinkled the corners of his eyes and exposed a mouthful of snow-white teeth.

"You mean, find a beautiful woman up in the mountains?"

The faint flare of her nostrils said she didn't appreciate his flirty question and Marshall inwardly sighed. He should have known the woman would be cool. Rich, pampered women usually were. The words friendly and down-to-earth probably weren't in her vocabulary.

"No. I mean rock climbing," she said a bit curtly.

"Oh. Well, actually I do quite a bit of climbing and hiking. Along with biking and kayaking. Once the snow leaves the slopes, that is."

She looked faintly interested and Marshall felt momentarily encouraged. Maybe the woman was approachable after all.

"You obviously like outdoor sports," she said.

"Yeah. Skiing is my first love. I could do that every day of the year. But of course, my wallet would get pretty empty if I didn't work once in a while," he added with a grin.

Like the flip of a light switch, her back went ramrod straight and her lips compressed to a tight line. Her gaze shifted from him to a magpie squawking from a branch on a nearby spruce tree. Apparently she preferred the bird's talk to his.

After a moment, she asked in a cool tone, "Or find a willing woman to pay for your sporting games."

Stunned - by this abrupt change in her, Marshall stared at her profile. She might look like an exotic princess, but that didn't mean he was going to let himself be insulted. Hadn't she ever heard of a joke?

"I beg your pardon?" he asked.

Her head swiveled back around and she stared down her straight little nose at him. "Oh, come on, I'm sure you do this all the time. Strike up innocent conversations with single women, turn on the charm and eventually get your hand in their pocketbook. Isn't that the way your game is played?"

So she thought he was after her money. Marshall was so incensed he would have very much liked to turn her over his knee and whack that pretty little bottom of hers until she apologized. But he wasn't about to use caveman tactics on a woman. She'd probably miss the point of a spanking anyway.

"Sorry, Ms.—uh—Smith, isn't it? Mia Smith?"

A mixture of surprise and suspicion suddenly crossed her face. "How do you know my name?"

"I'm Marshall Cates—the staff doctor for Thunder Canyon Resort. I've heard your name mentioned by some of the other staffers. And in case you didn't know, there are people, like me, who can make it just fine in life without a pile of riches. My salary easily takes care of my wants. I certainly don't need a woman to take care of me financially," he added coolly.

Completely stunned now, Mia stared at the man standing a few steps away. She'd assumed he was also a guest at the resort. She'd jumped to conclusions and figured he'd heard she was a single woman with money and thought she would probably be an easy prey to his good looks. To learn that he was a doctor at the resort—no doubt a well-to-do one—both rattled and embarrassed her.

Hot color washed across her face as her fingertips flew up to press against her lips. Too bad she hadn't kept them shut earlier, she thought. No telling what the man was thinking of her.

"Oh, I—I'm sorry, Dr. Cates. I don't know what else to say." Glancing away from him she let out a loud, inward groan. Why couldn't she do anything right anymore? Is that what inheriting money had done to her? Turned her into a mistrustful snob?

Drawing in a deep, bracing breath, she turned her gaze back to him and once again felt the jolt of the man's presence. He wasn't just a good-looking guy in a pair of sweaty shorts and T-shirt. He was so masculine that she could almost feel the sexuality seeping from him. Waves of coffee-brown hair naturally streaked by the sun were tousled around his head. Eyes the color of a chocolate bar peered at her from beneath thick, hooded brows. A straight nose flared slightly over a pair of lips that at the moment were compressed into a tight, angry line. A faint shadow of evening stubble covered a strong jaw and a chin that jutted proudly forward, telling her more about his personality than his words.

At the moment he appeared to be waiting for her to explain the meaning of her insulting comments and she supposed he deserved that much from her. Yet how could she really explain without telling the man things about her that she didn't want anyone to know?

"I thought— I took it for granted that you were a guest, Dr. Cates, and I was afraid— Well, you see I've had to deal with the problem of men…approaching me for financial reasons." Her features crumpled with remorse. "I'm sorry I was so quick to misjudge you. Please accept my apology."

He continued to study her with a guarded eye and Mia realized he was weighing her words and her sincerity. She couldn't blame him for that. Even so, she didn't know why his opinion of her should matter so much. She wasn't at Thunder Canyon Resort to find herself a man, even a respectable man like Dr. Cates. In fact, she'd run almost blindly to this area of Montana, hoping that no one from her past would be able to follow. She'd come here seeking peace and privacy, nothing more.

"I'm curious, Ms. Smith. Just exactly what is it about me that made you think I was a gigolo?"

More hot color washed up her neck and over her face and her gaze dropped guiltily to the toes of her hiking boots. "There wasn't— You don't look like a gigolo, Dr. Cates. I guess it was that flirty line about finding a beautiful woman in the mountains that set my alarm bell off."

She glanced up to see the doctor folding his arms across his chest while studying her with curious amusement.

"I'm sure a woman like you runs into flirty men on a daily basis. I hope you don't insult them all the way you just did me."

So he wasn't going to make this easy for

her, Mia thought. Well, it didn't matter. She had apologized to him. He could accept her offer or not. Either way, she'd probably never see the man again.

Stifling a sigh, she reached up and shoved back a strand of hair being tossed about by a lazy wind. "Look, Dr. Cates, I've apologized. There's not much more I can say."

He grinned at her in much the same way that he had earlier and, in spite of the rigid resistance she'd been trying to hold onto, she felt herself drawn to the man.

He said, "Except that you'll walk down the mountain with me."

His offhand invitation took her by surprise. Even though that flirty smile of his was aimed straight at her, she wasn't expecting him to take this meeting between them a step further. And though her first instinct was to withdraw and tell him she preferred her privacy, the feminine side of her was intrigued and flattered by his overture.

"That is," he added, "if you are ready to leave the mountain. I wouldn't want to rush you away from this spot. Not after the laboring hike it took to get up here."

The idea that he appreciated her physical effort to climb to this particular shelf of the mountain warmed her even more and she found herself smiling back at him.

"It was quite a trek for me to make it this far," she admitted. Twisting around, she bent down and picked up a small backpack lying at the base of the boulder. As she shouldered it on, she said, "But I am ready to go. The sun is beginning to dip."

"Great," he said with a smile. "Just let me get my things and we'll head down the trail together."

Mia followed him over to the rock ledge and waited while he shoved his climbing equipment into a vary large backpack. After he'd secured the straps over his shoulders, he gestured toward the direction of the trail.

"Shall we go?"

Nodding, Mia fell in step with him and was immediately staggered by his nearness. Since less than a foot separated their shoulders, she was close enough to pick up the faint spicy scent of cologne mingled with sweat, an odor that was extremely masculine, even erotic. And for the first time in ages, Mia found her senses distracted by a man.

"I guess getting outdoors is a nice break from working in an office," she commented as they picked their way down the rocky trail.

"I'd go crazy if I couldn't get out and do something physical," he told her. "But I do enjoy being a doctor."

She glanced at him from the corner of her eye. Looking at his lean body, Mia could plainly see he got plenty of strenuous exercise. His arms and legs were roped with hard muscles.

"Are you a general practitioner?"

A hint of amusement grooved his cheeks and Mia couldn't help but wonder about his odd reaction to her question. Did he think being a general practitioner was a joke? She hated to think he was one of those specialists that went around with their nose up in the air.

"No. There's not much need for one of those at the resort. I specialize in sports medicine. Twisted ankles, broken bones, strained muscles and pulled tendons. We have lots of skiers and hikers here."

For some reason, she could easily imagine him examining a blond ski bunny's strained leg. She'd bet a pile of money that the majority of his patients were female. But she wasn't about to suggest such a thing to Dr. Cates. She'd already stuck one foot in her mouth this afternoon. Mia wasn't about to try for a second.

"What about sniffles and fever? Can you treat those, too?"

He tossed her a wide grin. "Sure I can. Why? You're not feeling ill, are you?"

Her nostrils flared at his suggestive question. "I feel very well, thank you. I was just wondering about those guests that might get colds or tummy aches."

He chuckled and Mia realized she liked the warm husky sound that rolled easily past his lips. It said he was happy with himself and his life. She was envious. Desperately envious.

"Well, wonder no more, Ms. Smith. I can do what any general practitioner can do, plus a little more."

The teeny thread of arrogance in his voice was just enough to give him an air of confidence rather than conceit. And she realized she liked that about him, liked the self-assurance he possessed. If only she could be that sure of her own abilities and decisions, she thought wistfully. Maybe then she could step out and begin to live again, instead of hiding herself here in Thunder Canyon.

"If that's the case, the resort must be getting a lot for their money."

He chuckled again. "I like to think so."

The trail suddenly turned a bit steep and treacherous, forcing them to focus on their steps rather than their conversation. But despite her best effort, Mia's boots slipped on the loose gravel.

Her arms were flailing about, snatching for any sort of bush to help her regain her balance, when she felt the doctor's arm wrap around her waist and his strong hand grip the side of her waist.

"Careful now," he said in a steadying voice. "I've got you."

Breathing deeply from the physical scramble to stay upright, she tucked her long hair behind her ears and darted a grateful glance at his face.

"Thanks," she murmured between quick breaths. "I…almost went over head first."

Their gazes collided and Mia felt as though everything around them were slowing to a crawl. Except for her heart, which suddenly seemed to be going at breakneck speed, pumping hot blood straight to her face.

"It would be a steep tumble from here," he said, his voice husky. "I'm glad that didn't happen."

His brown eyes left hers and began to glide over her face as though they were fingers reverently touching a beautiful flower. The idea so unsettled Mia that she nervously swallowed and looked away from him.

Tall, pungent spruce along with white-barked aspen grew right to the edge of the hiking trail. The branches blocked out the sun, making it appear later in the evening than it really was and leaving Mia feeling as though the two of them were cocooned in their own little world. She wasn't ready for that much togetherness with a man who took her breath away each time she looked at him.

"Uh, we should be going," she quickly suggested. "The shadows are getting longer."

"Let me go first so I can help you down this rough patch," he told her.

To her relief he released his hold on her waist and carefully eased down the path a few feet in front of her. Once he found solid footing, he reached a hand up to her.

"Take my hand. I don't want you to fall."

She could have sat on her rump and scooted down the washed out part of the trail, but that would have been a little humiliating to do in front of a man who climbed mountains. Besides, he was only watching out for her safety, not merely trying to find an excuse to touch her, she told herself.

Leaning forward, she latched her fingers around his and with a firm grip he steadied her as she maneuvered over the last few treacherous steps.

"Thanks," she told him. "I've got to admit I was dreading going over this area again. I had to practically crawl on my way up."

He nodded. "I think this washout needs to be reported. The resort has maintenance people for repairing just this sort of thing. It might save a guest from a bad injury."

Mia suddenly realized he was still holding her hand and she was letting him.

Feeling like a naive teenager, she disengaged her fingers from his and carefully stepped around him. To her relief, he didn't try to delay her. Instead, he followed a few steps behind her.

She was trying hard to focus on the trail and the birds flittering among the limbs of the aspens, rather than the man behind her, when his voice suddenly sounded again.

"Are you a Montana native?"

His question put her on instant alert. If his questions grew too personal she didn't know how she could evade them without coming off as snobbish.

"No. Actually, I'm from Colorado."

"Oh. Then you're used to the mountains," he casually commented.

Truthfully, she'd grown up in a southern area of the state where most of the land was flat and used for farming and ranching. But that was more information than she wanted to give this man. He might inadvertently say something to other employees at the resort and if Janelle, her mother, just happened to be searching for her, the information might put the woman on her trail. And seeing Janelle right now was the very last thing Mia wanted in her life.

"Well, you could say I'm used to gazing at them from afar. I…uh, live in Denver."

He chuckled. "There're hundreds of beautiful vacation spots all over your state and you chose to come to Thunder Canyon. I'm amazed."

Put like that it did sound strange, even ridiculous. But she wasn't about to explain her motives for coming to Montana. Dr. Cates was obviously a man with wealth and prestige, maybe even a family. He would be outraged if he knew the real Mia. Mia Hanover. Not Mia Smith. That name was just as phony as the person she was trying to be.

Stifling a sigh, she said, "I'd never been up here. I wanted to see more of the state than just pictures."

Her simple excuse sounded reasonable enough. Lord only knew it was a mistake for a man to try to understand the workings of a woman's mind. Still, something about Mia

Smith being here didn't feel right to him. Even so, he wasn't going to press her with any more questions. Something about the clipped edge to her words told him not to pry, at least, for right now.

"I'm glad you did. I hope you're having a nice stay," he told her. "Do you have plans to stay much longer?"

Long moments passed without any sort of reply from her and Marshall had decided she was going to ignore his question completely when she suddenly paused on the trail and looked over her shoulder at him.

"I'm…not sure. I'm taking things a day at a time."

A day at a time? Most normal folks went on vacation with a planned date of arrival and departure. They allotted themselves a certain amount of time for fun and mentally marked a day to go home. Work, school and other responsibilities demanded a timetable. But then Mia Smith wasn't like "normal folks." She was obviously rich. She didn't have responsibilities, he reminded himself. More than likely she was a lady of leisure. She didn't have to worry about getting back to a job.

She's out of your league, Marshall. You'd do well to remember that.

The tiny voice running through his head made sense. But it also irked him. He wasn't a man who always wanted to play it safe. He liked excitement and pleasure and getting to know Mia Smith would definitely give him both.

The next five minutes passed in silence as the two of them carefully made their way to the bottom shelf of the mountain. Here the ground flattened somewhat and the trail they'd been traveling split, with one path looping by the river before it headed back to the resort. The other trail was a more direct path to the ski lodge.

Shifting his backpack to a more comfortable position, Marshall paused at the intersection of trails to look at her.

"Would you like to walk down by the river?"

Her gaze skittered over his face before it finally settled on the horizon. Even before she spoke a word, Marshall could feel her putting distance between them.

"Sorry, but I have a few things I need to do back at my cabin. In fact, if you'll excuse me, I think I'll get on down the trail." She reached to briefly shake his hand. "Thank you for helping me with the trip down. Goodbye."

Before Marshall could make any sort of

reply, she quickly turned and headed down the beaten path that would lead her back to the lodge.

Amused by her abrupt departure, Marshall stared after Mia Smith, while wondering where he'd gone wrong. He wasn't accustomed to women walking away from him. In fact, most of the time he had to think up some polite excuse to get rid of unwanted advances.

Mia Smith had just given him a dose of his own medicine and though the idea should have had him throwing his head back and laughing at the irony of it all, he could do nothing but stare down the trail after her and wonder if he would ever have the chance to talk with her again.

Chapter Two

Thunder Canyon Resort's infirmary was a set of rooms located on the bottom floor at the back of the massive lodge. When Caleb Douglas, wealthy businessman and cattle baron of Thunder Canyon, decided to build the resort, he'd spared no expense. The multistories of wood and glass spread across the slope of mountain like a modern-day castle. By itself, Marshall's office was large enough to hold a Saturday night dance. In fact, he'd often thought how perfect the gleaming hardwood floors would be for boot scootin' and twirling a pretty girl under his arm. Not very professional thoughts for a doctor, Marshall supposed, but then he hardly had the job of a normal doctor.

One whole wall of his office was constructed of glass; it was an enormous window to the outside world. His desk, a huge piece of gleaming cherrywood, had been placed at the perfect angle for Marshall to view the nearby mountains and a portion of the ski slope. At this time in the summer, it wasn't rare for him to look up from his paperwork to see elk or mule deer grazing along the slopes.

Yes, it was a cushy job. One that Marshall had never dreamed of having. At least not while he'd been trudging through medical school, burning the midnight oil over anatomy books while his friends were out partying.

When Marshall had finally received his doctorate, he'd come home and taken a job at Thunder Canyon General Hospital. At the time some of his friends had wondered about his choice. They had all continually reminded him that his specialty in sports medicine could possibly open up big doors for him. Wouldn't he like to work for a major league team in baseball or the NFL where he could make piles of money?

Marshall would be the first to admit that he

liked money and he'd gone into the medical profession believing it was a way to make a fortune without breaking his back. But he hadn't necessarily had his eye on a job that would take him away from his hometown.

By the time he'd finished medical school and his internship, he'd been too homesick to even consider going off to some major city on the East or West Coast to look for a job. Instead, he'd returned to Thunder Canyon, never dreaming that his hometown was about to undergo a sudden and drastic change.

A little over two years ago the discovery of gold at the Queen of Hearts mine had quickly changed the whole area. Businesses, mostly catering to tourists, were sprouting up in Thunder Canyon like daffodils in springtime. The resort, which had started out as a single lodge with a ski slope, had expanded to an upscale, year-round tourist attraction with all sorts of indoor and outdoor enticements for the young and old. And the resort was continuing to build and expand. Under the management of Marshall's longtime buddy Grant Clifton, the recreational hot spot had become a gold mine itself. And Marshall was definitely reaping part of the rewards.

This morning, as soon as he'd entered his

office, his assistant Ruthann had placed a steaming cup of coffee along with a plate of buttered croissants on his desk. The woman had been a registered nurse for nearly thirty years and three years ago had just settled into retirement when her husband suddenly died of a heart attack. The tragedy had put her in financial straits and when Marshall had heard she'd needed a job, he'd decided she'd be perfect as his assistant.

Now after a year of working with her, he realized he'd been more than right about the woman. She was an excellent nurse with plenty of experience, plus he didn't have to worry about her ogling him as something to take home to meet mother. In fact, in her early fifties, Ruthann was more like a mother to him than an assistant.

"Surprise, surprise. You actually have three patients this morning," she said with dry amusement as she watched him chomp into one of the croissants. "Any clue as to when you'd like to see them?"

"Are any of them critical?" he asked, even though he knew if any patient had arrived with serious injuries, Ruthann wouldn't be standing around gabbing.

"A sprained ankle, a cut knee and a jammed

finger. I think the finger case is just a ruse to see you. She's young and blond and drenched with designer perfume."

"What a suspicious mind you have, Ruthie," he scolded playfully.

Her laugh was mocking. "I see the sort of games that go on in this infirmary. Frankly, it amazes me how brazen women can be nowadays when it comes to you men."

The memory of Mia Smith's aloof, even shy behavior toward him yesterday had been something entirely different from the sort of women Ruthann was describing. Maybe that's why he couldn't get the heiress out of his mind.

"Okay, Ruthie, I'll forget my breakfast and go see if Ms. Blonde really has a finger problem."

The petite woman with short red hair and a face full of freckles snorted with playful sarcasm. "That's no way for a doctor to eat."

Grinning, he retorted, "Then why did you put it here for me?"

"Because I knew you'd sleep instead of get out of bed and make yourself breakfast."

Marshall shook a finger at her. "I'll have you know I was up early this morning. I just didn't make breakfast because I was chasing Leroy halfway down the mountain. He dug a hole last night beneath the backyard fence. Guess he was mad at me for not taking him hiking yesterday."

Marshall's Australian blue heeler was often so adept at understanding his master that it was downright eerie. No matter how he tried, Marshall couldn't fool the dog.

"You went hiking? I thought you were going to help your dad paint that workshed of his."

Shaking his head, Marshall wiped bread crumbs from his fingers and picked up the three files Ruthann had placed in front of them. Since they all belonged to current guests of the lodge, each of the manila folders held only a single sheet inside them. Being a doctor at a place where people resided for only a few days or weeks didn't allow the opportunity to make longtime patients. Temperature and blood-pressure readings didn't tell him much about a person. But that was okay with Marshall. He'd never set out to be one of those kind family doctors who knew all the townsfolk by name, made sure they kept all their routine checkups and often served as their counselor and therapist. That sort of doctoring took commitment and he was too busy enjoying himself in other ways to chain himself to an office.

"He and Mom had to do something with

some friends—something about an anniversary celebration. We've planned the painting day for another time."

He rose to his feet, a signal to Ruthann that it was time for them to get to work. As they walked to the door, he said casually, "I met the heiress yesterday."

Pausing, Ruthann twisted her head around to give him a bemused look. "The heiress," she repeated blankly. "What are you talking about?"

He rolled his eyes. Normally Ruthann was the one who kept him up on resort guests. He couldn't believe she was unaware of Mia Smith.

"*The heiress.* You know, that black-haired beauty that everyone has been talking about. The one that's always alone."

Ruthann's brows suddenly lifted with dawning. "Oh, that one. I didn't realize she was an heiress. Where'd you get that information?"

"Well, I don't know for a fact that she's an heiress. Grant was the one who insinuated that she must be from a rich family. She's been here more than two weeks now. Only a person with money to spare could afford that much time at a luxury resort. He said she rented a safety deposit box for her jewels, too."

"Grant! Isn't he supposed to be engaged to Stephanie? What's he doing gossiping about a female guest?"

Marshall sighed. Yep, Ruthann was just like a mother, he decided, maybe worse. "Don't go jumping to the wrong conclusions. I was the one asking Grant about Mia Smith."

Ruthann shot him a frown of disgust. "I should have guessed." She clucked her tongue in a disapproving way. "A grown man, a doctor at that, prying for information about a woman you don't know from Adam. Shame on you, Marshall Cates. Now what was she like?"

Marshall laughed at the nurse's abrupt turn-around on the sins of gossiping. "Cool. Very cool," he told her. "But as pretty as the rising sun. I got the sense, though, that she's like that beautiful actress, uh—" he paused as his mind searched for the name "—Greta Garbo. She wants to be alone."

Nodding shrewdly the nurse said, "In other words she didn't fall for any of your nonsense."

Reaching for the doorknob, Marshall yanked it open and taking Ruthann by the shoulder ushered her over the threshold.

"Don't count me out yet, Ruthie. Besides, for all you know the woman has been pacing her room, wondering how she can get a second chance with me."

Ruthann chuckled. "I'm sure she's tearing her hair out for an opportunity to get her hands on you."

That was the last thing Mia Smith was probably doing, Marshall thought wryly. But then he wasn't going to let her snub get to him. He'd never had to beg or cajole any woman into having a date with him and he'd be a fool to start now.

With a good-natured chuckle, he nudged Ruthann on toward the first examining room. "Let her pine. Why would I need a beautiful heiress when I have you?"

Behind the lodge, several hundred feet farther up the mountain, Mia paced through the suite of rooms she'd been living in since she'd arrived at Thunder Canyon Resort. A day ago she had considered the luxurious log cabin as a refuge. But now, after the encounter on the mountain with Dr. Marshall Cates, her peace of mind had been shattered.

She'd gone there hoping the quietness and the beauty would allow her to meditate, maybe even help her decide what to do next with her life. But then *he* showed up and her senses had been blown away by his charming smile and strong, masculine presence.

Now she was afraid to step out of her cabin and especially leery of walking down to the lodge, where the infirmary was located. The lodge meant maybe running into Dr. Cates and Mia didn't want to risk seeing him again. He was trouble. She'd felt it when she'd first looked into his eyes and felt her heart race like a wild mustang galloping across a grassy plain.

So what are you going to do, Mia? Stay in your cabin for the next month?

Groaning with self-disgust, Mia sank onto a wide window seat that looked down upon the lodge and the cluster of numerous other resort buildings, imagining what it would look like in the dead of winter. Everything would be capped with white snow and skiers would be riding the lifts and playing on the slopes.

Suddenly, her cell phone rang, the shrill sound jangling her nerves. She stared warily at the small instrument lying on an end table.

There were only a handful of people that had her number and she'd left all of them behind in Colorado. She'd told what few friends she had that she was taking an extended vacation and didn't know when she might return. As for her mother, Mia hadn't told

Janelle Josephson anything. She'd simply left the woman a note telling her that she was going away for a while and to please give her the space she needed.

That had been nearly three weeks ago, and Janelle had rang Mia's cell phone every day since. And every day Mia had refused to take her call.

Mercifully, the ringing finally stopped and Mia left the window seat to look at the caller ID. Just as she expected. Janelle wouldn't give up. She wanted to be a part of her daughter's life. And as much as Mia hated to reject her, right now she couldn't even think of Janelle as her mother. As far as she was concerned her mother was dead and nothing, not even a pile of money, would ever bring her back.

There are people, like me, who make it just fine in life without a pile of riches.

Dr. Marshall Cates' words had pierced her heart like a flaming arrow and even a day later they continued to haunt her, to remind her of the awful, selfish choices she'd made in her life.

Money. She desperately wished that she'd never needed or wanted it. She wanted to take what she had of it and throw it into the nearest river. At least then maybe she would feel clean.

At least then maybe she could start over. But something told her that even that drastic measure wouldn't heal the wounds she was carrying.

Angry with herself, she put down the phone, walked over to the dining table and grabbed the handbag she'd tossed there earlier. Seeking privacy didn't mean she had to totally hide from life. And if she did cross paths with Dr. Marshall Cates, she could handle it. After all, he was just a man.

A man who would look at you with disgust if he knew you'd once been Mia Hanover, a woman who'd killed her own mother.

For a brief moment, Mia shut her eyes tightly and swallowed hard as the memory of Nina Hanover's death filled her mind like a dark cloud. Her adoptive mother had been a woman who'd worked hard as a farmer's wife, who'd always tried to give Mia the best in life. She'd been a sweet, loving woman until the alcohol had taken her into its awful grip.

With a groan of anguish, Mia shook her head and hurried out of the cabin, wallowing in guilt and self-pity wasn't going to fix anything. She had to get out and get her mind on other things.

A half hour later, in downtown Thunder Canyon, she parked her rental car in front of the Clip 'N' Curl. Even though Mia had made use of the fancy beauty salon and spa located on the resort, she felt much more comfortable here in this traditional, down-home beauty parlor. Here the women dressed casually and everyone talked as though they were all family.

Since the majority of the women at the resort appeared to use the Aspenglow for their beauty treatments, Mia figured the patrons of the Clip 'N' Curl were local residents. In fact, a few days ago when she'd visited the place, she'd heard a couple of the women complaining about the traffic problems that the influx of tourists had brought to Thunder Canyon.

Since Mia was one of those tourists, she'd simply sat quietly and listened to the other customers discussing the Queen of Hearts mine and how the recent discovery of gold there had turned the town topsy-turvy. Several of the women felt that the new money was a wonderful thing for the little town, but others had spoken about how much they hated the traffic, the crowds and the loss of Thunder Canyon's quaintness.

Money. Gold. Riches. The subject seemed to follow Mia no matter where she went. If she could manage a walk-in appointment today, she hoped the shoptalk would be about something different. The last thing she wanted to think about was the money Janelle, her birth mother, had showered upon her and how drastically it had changed Mia's once simple life.

Leaving her small rental car, Mia walked into the Clip 'N' Curl and waited at the front desk. The small salon was presently undergoing major renovations. Only three stations were up and working amid the chaos of working carpenters. And today all three styling chairs were full while only three empty chairs remained in the small waiting area.

Figuring she'd never get an appointment, Mia turned to leave the shop when one of the hairdressers called out to her.

"Don't leave, honey. We'll make a place for you. Just have a seat. There's free coffee and muffins if you'd like a snack while you wait."

"Thank you. I'll be glad to wait," Mia told her, then took a seat in one of the empty plastic chairs.

As Mia reached forward and picked up one of the style magazines lying on a coffee table, the woman sitting next to her said, "Your hair looks beautiful. I hope you're not planning to cut it."

Easing back in the chair, Mia glanced over to see it was a college-aged woman who'd given her the compliment. Short, feathery spikes of chestnut hair framed a round face while a friendly smile spread a pair of wide lips.

Mia smiled back at her. "No. Just a shampoo and blow-dry. I've tried short hair before and believe me I didn't look nearly as cute as you."

The young woman let out a quiet, bubbly laugh. "Thanks for the compliment, but compared to you I'm just a plain Jane." She thrust her hand over toward Mia. "Hi, I'm Marti Newmar."

Mia shook Marti's hand and as she did she realized it had been months, maybe longer since she'd felt a real need to communicate with another woman just for the sake of talking and sharing ideas. Dear God, maybe this quaint little western town was beginning to help her heal, she thought.

"Mia Smith. Nice to meet you."

Marti's nose wrinkled at the tip as she thoughtfully studied Mia. "I think I've seen you somewhere. You live around here?"

Trying to push away the cloak of wariness she constantly wore, Mia said, "No. I'm a guest at Thunder Canyon Resort."

Marti's lips parted in an *O*, then her fingers snapped with sudden recognition. "That's it.

That's where I've seen you. In the resort lounge."

Mia relaxed. She should have known this young woman had to be a local and not someone from Denver or Alamosa, Colorado, where she'd lived for most of her adult life.

"Yes, that's probably where it was," Mia agreed.

"I just started working at the coffee shop in the lounge a few days ago." She laughed. "I'm still learning how to make a latte. I grew up on a nearby ranch and the only kind of coffee my parents ever drank was the cowboy kind. You know, throw the grounds and water into a granite pot and let it boil. This fancy stuff is all new to me."

Warmed by the woman's openness, Mia smiled at her. "I'm sure you'll learn fast."

"I hope so. Grant Clifton, the guy that manages the resort, was kind enough to give me a job doing something. You see, I'm trying to get through college and the cost is just awful. I got a partial scholarship on my grades and this job should help with the rest of the expense."

Marti's situation was so familiar to Mia that she almost felt as though she were looking in a mirror. Five years ago she'd entered college with hopes of getting a degree in nursing. But at that time her father had already passed away and, using what little money she and her mother could earn at menial jobs, she'd had to settle for taking one or two classes at a time. Those years had been very rough and discouraging. It had been during those terribly lean times in her life that her priorities had gone haywire. She'd begun to think that money could fix everything that was messed up in her life. She'd been so very, very wrong.

"Whatever you do, don't give up," Mia encouraged her. "It may take you a while to find your dream, but you will."

Nodding, Marti said, "Yeah, that's what my mother keeps telling me." Tilting her head to one side, she continued to study Mia. "Have you met many people at the resort?"

The young woman's question instantly brought the image of Marshall Cates to Mia's mind.

"A few. I'm not…much of a social person."

"Hmm. Well, there're all sorts of good-looking men hanging around there." She gave Mia an impish grin. "But I only think of them as eye candy. I'm not about to let some smooth-tongued devil change my plans to become a teacher."

"I'm sure some day you'll want to marry.

When the time is right for you," Mia told Marti, while wondering if that time would ever come for herself. At one time, Mia had dreamed and hoped for a family of her own. Now she would just settle for some sort of peace to come to her heart. Otherwise she'd never be able to give her love to anyone.

Marti shrugged in a ho-hum way. "I don't know. I've seen my older sister get her heart-broken over and over again." She looked at Mia. "You know Dr. Cates? The hunk that works at the resort?"

Every nerve in Mia's body suddenly went on alert. What was she going to learn about the man now?

"Vaguely," she said, not about to elaborate on the surprise encounter she'd had with the man.

Marti sighed, telling Mia that the young woman definitely considered Marshall Cates eye candy. "Gorgeous, isn't he?"

"He's, uh—a nice-looking man."

"Mmm. Well, my sister, Felicia, thought so, too. They dated for a while and she was getting wedding bells on the brain."

Mia was afraid to ask, but she did anyway. "What happened?"

Wrinkling her nose, Marti said, "She found

out the good doctor wasn't about to settle for just one woman. Not when he had a flock of them waiting in line."

So the man was a playboy. That shouldn't surprise her. No matter where he was or who he was with, the man was bound to turn female heads. The best thing she could do was forget she'd ever met him. Still, she couldn't help but ask the question, "Is your sister still dating Dr. Cates?"

Marti chuckled. "No, thank goodness. She finally opened her eyes wide where Marshall Cates was concerned. She recently moved to Bozeman and got engaged to another guy."

Across the room, one of the hairdressers called out. "Marti, I'm ready for you, honey."

Smiling at Mia, the young woman hurriedly snatched up her handbag and jumped to her feet. "Nice meeting you, Mia. Maybe I'll see you at the coffee shop. Come by and say hello, okay?"

Nodding, Mia returned Marti's smile. "Sure. I'll look forward to it."

Later that afternoon, at the resort lodge, Marshall finished up the small amount of paperwork he had to do, then left Ruthann in charge of the quiet infirmary and headed down to the lounge bar for a short break.

Three couples were sitting at tables, busy talking and sipping tall, cool drinks. One older man with graying hair and a hefty paunch was sitting at the end of the bar. He appeared to be sleeping off his cocktail.

Lizbeth Stanton was tending bar this afternoon, and the pretty young woman with long auburn hair smiled when Marshall slid onto one of the stools.

"Hey, there. I was about to decide you weren't going to show up today." She glanced at the watch on her wrist. "This is late for you."

Marshall chuckled. "I'm so relieved that at least one woman around this place is interested enough to keep up with my comings and goings."

She shot him a sexy smile. "Awww. Poor Marshall," she cooed. "Had a bad day?"

With an easy grin, he raked a hand through his dark, wavy hair.

"I've never seen so many patients in one day. Several were suffering from altitude sickness and one had taken a nasty fall on a hiking trail. But they'll all be okay."

Not bothering to ask if he wanted a drink, Lizbeth went over to a back bar and began to mix him a cherry cola. At one end of the work counter, a small stereo was emitting the twangy sounds of a popular country music tune.

"Well," Lizbeth said to him, "that *is* what you're paid for. To doctor people who have more money than sense."

Yeah, he thought, that's right. But sometimes in the darkest part of the night, when everything looks different, he wondered if he was just as shallow as some of the guests he treated. He'd not gone to school for eight years intending to doctor women who'd ripped off nail beds trying to rock climb with false fingernails. But on the other hand, Marshall was making an enormous salary and most days he hardly had to lift a hand to earn it. He'd be crazy to want anything else. Wouldn't he?

Lizbeth carried the tall glass over to the bar and placed it on a cork coaster before she pushed the frosty drink in front of him.

"Here, since you can't drink anything alcoholic on the job, maybe this will perk you up."

"Thanks, beautiful. Remind me to do something for you sometime." Giving her a wink, he took a sip of the drink, then lifted the stemmed cherry she'd placed on top and popped it into his mouth.

As he chewed the sweet treat, Lizbeth's brown eyes studied him in a calculating way.

"Well, if you really mean that you could take me out to dinner tonight. I'm getting tired of taking home a sack of fast food and eating it in front of the television."

Marshall chuckled a second time. He doubted Lizbeth ever had to spend a night alone, unless she wanted it that way. Even if she was known as a big flirt, she was pretty, bubbly and enjoyable to be around, the perfect type of woman for Marshall, who didn't want any sort of clingy hands grabbing hold of him.

"If you'd really like to go out to dinner tonight, then I'm all for it."

A faint look of surprise crossed her face. "You really mean that?"

Marshall shrugged. He and Lizbeth both knew that neither of them would ever be serious about each other, but that didn't mean they couldn't enjoy an evening together. Besides, eating dinner with a warm, appreciative female was better than being snubbed by a cool, beautiful heiress.

"Sure," he answered. "Let's splurge and eat at the Gallatin Room. The grilled salmon is delicious."

Lizbeth's brown eyes were suddenly sparkling and Marshall wondered what it would take to see Mia Smith react to him in such a way.

Damn it, man, forget the woman, Marshall scolded himself. You've got plenty of female distraction around here. You don't need to get hung up on a woman who's apparently forgotten how to smile.

"Oh, this is great, Marshall! I can wear my new high heels. Just for you," she added with coy sweetness. "What time shall we meet?"

"When do you get off work?" Marshall asked.

"Six this evening. But I can ready by seven."

"Okay, I'll meet you in the lounge at seven-thirty," he told her. And by then he was going to make damn sure that the winsome Mia Smith was going to be pushed completely out of his thoughts.

Chapter Three

Mia wasn't at all sure why she'd bothered going out to eat this evening, especially at the Gallatin Room. Before she'd found Janelle, Mia had never been inside a restaurant where the tables were covered with fine linen and the food was served on fragile china. After her father, Will Hanover, had died of a lung disease, she and her mother had been lucky to splurge on burgers and fries at the local fast-food joint. The sort of life she was experiencing here at Thunder Canyon Resort was the sort she could only dream about back then.

Today at the Clip 'N' Curl, her brief visit

with Marti Newmar had reminded her even more of how simple and precious those years on the farm had been with her adoptive parents. Maybe she'd not had much in the way of material things, but she'd been wrapped in the security of her family's loving arms. Mia had learned at an early age that she was adopted; yet that hadn't mattered. She'd been a happy girl until her father had died. And then things had gotten tough and she'd made all sorts of wrong choices. She'd begun to believe that money was all it would take to fix everything wrong in her life. Well, now she had it, but she was far from happy.

With a wistful sigh, she realized the Gallatin Room was the sort of restaurant that a woman should visit with her husband or lover. The small table where Mia sat near a wall of plate glass gave a magnificent view of the riding stables and several corrals of beautiful horses. Far beyond, near the valley floor, a river glistened like a ribbon of silver in the moonlight. Yet the pleasant sights couldn't hold Mia's attention. Instead she was imagining what it would be like if the handsome Dr. Cates was sitting opposite her, reaching across the fine white linen and clasping her fingers with his.

"Ms. Smith, your steak will be ready in a few minutes. Would you like more wine?"

Mia looked around to see a young waiter hovering at her elbow, willing to jump through hoops, if necessary, to please her. After the first few days at Thunder Canyon Resort, Mia had become aware that some of the male staff seemed to bend over backward in an effort to make her happy. She'd not been fooled into thinking they were at her beck and call because they liked their job. No doubt they'd heard gossip or simply assumed that she was rich. The fact that she *was* rich, only made her resent their behavior even more.

"Yes, I will take more wine, thank you," she told him.

The young man filled Mia's goblet with the dark, fruity wine she'd selected, then eased back from the table. As he moved from her sight, Mia got a glimpse of movement from the corner of her eye. Turning her head slightly to the right, she was shocked to see the handsome doctor and a sexy redhead taking their seats several tables over from hers.

Mia stared for a moment, then purposely looked away before either of them could spot her. She'd seen the redhead before, but where?

Recognition hit her almost immediately. She

was the bartender here at the lounge. Mia had
visited the bar on a few occasions, just to enjoy
a cocktail and a change of scenery from the
rooms of her cabin. The redhead had always
been working behind the bar, but Mia had
never seen Dr. Cates there. Were the two of
them an item? It certainly appeared that way to
Mia. But from what Marti Newmar had told
her at the Clip 'N' Curl earlier today, the man
liked women in the plural form. The bartender
was probably just one in a long line waiting for
a date with Dr. Smooth.

Across the room, at Marshall's table, he and
Lizbeth had ordered and the waiter was
pouring chilled Chablis into Lizbeth's
stemmed glass when he looked slightly to the
left and spotted *the* woman. She was sitting
alone and, even over the heads of the other
diners, Marshall couldn't mistake the black-
haired beauty. It was Mia Smith, wearing a
slim pink sheath and black high heels with a
strap that fastened around her ankles. Her black
hair was swept tightly back from the perfect
oval of her face and knotted into an intricate
chignon at the back of her head. She was a
picture of quiet elegance and Marshall found
it hard not to stare.

"Dining here in this posh part of the resort

is quite a treat for me, Marshall. You must be feeling generous," Lizbeth teased.

Jerking his head back to his date, Marshall plastered a smile on his face. Lizbeth was the sort of woman who'd be happy to let a rich man take care of her for the rest of her life. Since it wasn't going to be him, he could afford to feel generous.

"Maybe I just felt as though I had earned my paycheck today," he told her.

She laughed. "Oh, Marshall, you're so funny at times. I hope you never go serious like that brother of yours. He should have been a judge."

Marshall had three brothers. At thirty, Mitchell was four years younger than him. And then there were the twins, Matthew and Marlon, who were just twenty-one and trying to finish up their last year of college.

At one time in their young lives both Marshall and Mitchell had walked somewhat on the wild side. And while the two boys had lived on the edge, they'd both loved a passel of ladies and broken more than a few hearts. But age had slowed both of them down, Mitchell especially. He'd founded a farm and ranching equipment business and spent nearly all his time making the place turn big dollars.

"That's why Mitchell has made a big success

of Cates International," Marshall said to her. "He takes his business seriously. When I'm out on the slopes skiing, he's usually at work. That's the difference between him and me."

Lizbeth playfully wrinkled her nose at him. "What's the use of money if you can't have a little fun with it?"

Marshall sipped at the beer he'd ordered, then licked the foam from his lips. He would surely like to ask Mia Smith that question, he thought. But then maybe she was having fun. Maybe being alone was how she liked things.

He looked back to the table where Mia was dining and before he could catch himself he was gazing at her again. At the moment she was eating one slow bite at a time. There was something very sensual in her movements, as though she was a woman who savored each and every taste. Marshall could only imagine what it would feel like to have those lush lips touching him.

"In case you don't know, her name is Mia Smith."

Lizbeth's comment doused him with hot embarrassment and he quickly jerked his attention back to his dining companion.

"You caught me. What can I say, Lizbeth, except that I'm sorry?"

Laughing lightly, she reached over and touched the top of his hand. "Don't bother. I know when a man considers me just a friend. It might be nice if you looked at me the way you're looking at her. But you don't."

Relief washed through him. Jealous women were hard to handle, especially in a place that required good manners. "Thanks for understanding, Lizbeth," he said wryly. "I guess I'm pretty transparent, huh?"

"Well, if I knew the Gettysburg address I would have had time enough to recite the whole thing while you were staring at Ms. Smith."

Shaking his head with a bit of self-disgust, he said, "I'm sorry. It's just that—well, I met her yesterday. On the mountain while I was hiking."

Intrigued by this morsel of news, Lizbeth leaned forward. "Really? Did you exchange words with the woman?"

The two of them had exchanged words, glances, even touches, but apparently none of it had affected Mia Smith the way it had Marshall. She'd walked away from him as though he were no more than a servant.

"A few."

"That's all? Just a few?"

"The lady is cool, Lizbeth. She—uh—wasn't interested in getting to know me."

Picking up her wineglass, Lizbeth laughed, which only caused the frown on Marshall's face to deepen. "That's hard to believe. I've talked with her at the bar and she seemed friendly to me."

Now it was Marshall's turn to stare with open curiosity at Lizbeth. "You know the woman?"

Shrugging, Lizbeth said, "She comes in the bar fairly often. Drinks a piña colada with only a dash of alcohol."

"Does she ever have anyone with her?"

"No. She's always alone," Lizbeth answered. "Can't figure it, can you? The lady is beautiful. Men would swoon at her feet, but apparently she won't let them. Maybe you ought to ask her for a date. If anyone can change her tune about the opposite sex, it would be you, dear Marshall."

He chuckled with disbelief. "Me? Not hardly. I offered to buy her a drink. She pretty much gave me the cold shoulder."

"Maybe you should try again. That is—if you're really interested in the woman."

Unable to stop himself, Marshall glanced over at Mia's table. At the moment she was staring pensively out the window as though she were seeking something in the starlit sky.

"Frankly, I wish I wasn't interested. I have a feeling the lady is trouble. She doesn't come across as the other rich guests around here. She's different."

Lizbeth smiled coyly. "And maybe that's why you can't get her off your mind. Because she *is* different."

He thoughtfully studied his date. "Hmm. Maybe you're right. And maybe once I got to know her, I'd find out she's not my type at all. Then I could safely cross her off my list."

Lizbeth let out a knowing little laugh. "You'll never know until you try."

The next morning on his way to work, Marshall entered the lodge by way of the lounge and headed to the coffee shop. After the busy day in the infirmary yesterday, he wanted to pick up one of those fancy lattes and present it to Ruthann when she walked through the door. No doubt the surprise treat would make his hardworking nurse want to whip out her thermometer and take his temperature, he thought wryly.

At this early hour, the coffee shop was full of customers sitting around the group of tiny tables, reading the *Thunder Canyon Nugget* and the daily newspaper from nearby Bozeman while drinking ridiculously expensive cups of flavored java. Marshall found himself waiting at the back of a long line and wondering if he had time to deal with getting the latte for Ruthann after all, when a vaguely familiar voice spoke behind him.

"Looks like we have a long line this morning."

Turning, he was more than surprised to see Mia Smith. She was dressed casually in jeans and a white shirt with the sleeves rolled back against her tanned arms. Her black hair was loose upon her shoulders and the strands glistened attractively in the artificial lights.

The sight of her put an instant smile on his face. "Yes. Everyone must have had the same idea for coffee this morning."

Mia could feel his gaze sliding over her face and down her throat to where her shirt made a V between her breasts. The sensual gaze made her wonder if he'd looked this same way at his date last night. Then just as quickly she scolded herself for speculating about the playboy doctor. The man's private behavior was none of her business.

Even so, she couldn't stop the next words out of her mouth. "How did you like your dinner last night at the Gallatin Room?"

His brows lifted ever so slightly. "I didn't realize you saw me there."

This morning he was obviously dressed for work in a pair of dark slacks and a baby-blue button-down shirt. A red tie with a blue geometric print was knotted neatly at his throat. She could see that he'd attempted to tame the wild waves of his thick hair, but several of the locks had already fallen onto his forehead. Just one look at him was probably enough to cure most of his female patients.

"I...uh—spotted you and your date when you were arriving."

"Oh. Well, Lizbeth wasn't actually a date. I mean—she was—but we're basically just friends. Actually, she was the one who asked me out."

Mia shot him a droll look. Was this the sort of line he handed out to all unsuspecting females?

"Good for her."

The line of customers began to move forward and she tried to peer around his shoulder to gauge how much longer the wait would be, but the man held her gaze.

"I stopped here at the coffee shop this morning to pick up a latte for my nurse," he explained. "She's always treating me so I thought I'd do something for her."

Figuring his nurse was a twenty-something blonde with long eyelashes and a come-hither smile, Mia said, "Why settle for just a coffee? Perhaps you should take her to the Gallatin Room, too."

To her amazement a look of dawning swept over his face and he nodded in agreement. "You know, that's a wonderful idea. Ruthann has been a nurse for more than thirty years and she's always taking care of other people, even when she isn't on the job. Her husband died of a heart attack about three years ago and she's having a hard time making ends meet with just his social security to help her along. Dinner at the Gallatin Room would be something really special for her. Thank you, Mia, for suggesting it."

Feeling suddenly like a heel, she hoped he never guessed that her suggestion had been given in sarcasm. Damn it, why did she continually want to believe this man was only out for himself? Because Marti had described him as a ladies' man? Or because a user could always spot another user, she thought dismally.

But you're not a user, Mia. Everything you have has been given to you freely. You haven't taken anything from anybody—except your adoptive mother's life.

Trying to shut away the guilty voice inside of her, Mia gave him a hesitant smile. "I—uh—think that would be a very nice gesture for your nurse."

"Well, I'm not always as thoughtful as I should be. Blame it on my male genes."

The grin on his handsome face was as wicked as the images going through Mia's head. She'd never been around a man who continually made her feel like she needed to take deep breaths of pure oxygen. Dr. Cates was making her think things that definitely belonged behind closed doors.

Smiling in spite of herself, she said, "I'm sure your nurse will think you're very thoughtful."

At that moment a customer carrying a portable cardboard holder filled with several cups of coffee was attempting to work his way through the crowd. As he jostled close to Mia, the doctor's hands closed around her shoulders and quickly set her out of the customer's path.

The abrupt movement brought her even closer to Marshall and he realized her thigh was pressed against his and the thrust of her breasts was almost touching his chest. His breathing slowed, while the faint scent of gardenia filled his head like a gentle breeze on a hot night.

"I—uh—thought that man's drink was going to topple right on you." Reluctantly, he eased his grip on her shoulders. "Sorry if I startled you."

He watched a pretty pink flush fill her cheeks. "I—it's okay. Better to be a little startled than scalded."

The line ahead of them moved again and Marshall quickly glanced over his shoulder to see he was next to place an order. If he was ever going to make his move on this woman he needed to do it now and fast.

"You— I noticed you were dining alone last night and I was wondering if you might like some company tonight? I'm free if you are."

Faint surprise crossed her face, an expression that puzzled Marshall. Surely a woman who looked like her was used to men asking her out to dinner.

"Actually, I don't think I could take the Gallatin Room two nights in a row. It's a little stuffy for my taste."

Hope sprang up in him like an exploding geyser and he wondered what the hell was coming over him. The world was full of pretty women and willing ones at that. Why had getting a date with this one suddenly become so important?

"Mine, too. I only took Lizbeth there because she— Well, she enjoys that sort of thing, but she can't really afford such a splurge on her own." Another quick glance over his shoulder told him the customer was about to step away from the counter. He turned a beseeching look on Mia. "We could go downtown and maybe grab a burger or pizza. How does that sound?"

She opened her mouth as though to speak, then just as quickly her pink lips pressed thoughtfully together. Behind him, the coffee shop attendant said, "Dr. Cates, it's your turn to order now."

With his eyes riveted on Mia's face, he tossed over his shoulder, "A large latte with plenty of foam."

His dark brown eyes were pulling her in, making her forget there was a crowd of people around them. In the back of her mind, she understood he was a man who would be dangerous to any woman's heart. Yet there was something about his smile that made him impossible to resist.

"Sure," she heard herself saying. "A burger would be nice."

"Great. Where shall I pick you up? Are you staying here in the lodge?"

Not yet ready to give him that much information, she said, "I'll meet you here at the lounge."

A wide smile suddenly dimpled both cheeks and Mia felt her insides go as gooey as warm taffy.

"Great. I'll be here. Six-thirty okay?"

Why not, she thought. It wasn't like she had anything important to do and maybe it was time she did something about this aimless path she'd been on for the past few months. "Six-thirty is fine. I'll see you then."

After he'd picked up his latte and given her a quick farewell, Mia found herself standing at the counter staring straight into Marti Newmar's smiling face.

"Hi, Mia! I didn't expect to see you here so soon. What can I get you this morning?"

"Hi yourself," Mia greeted the bubbly young woman. "I'd like a cappuccino with sugar and a pecan Danish."

Marti repeated the order to another worker who was busily preparing the drinks and rang in Mia's purchases.

While they waited on the cappuccino, Marti leaned slightly over the counter and said in a hushed voice, "Looks like Dr. Cates has his eye on you. Be careful, Mia. I wouldn't want you to end up like my sister."

Shaking her head, Mia smiled at the young woman's earnest face. "Don't worry, Marti. I'm not about to let the doctor turn my head."

"Yeah, well that's what Felicia said, too."

Thankfully, a worker set her order on the counter and Mia quickly scooped it up. Now that she'd agreed to a date with Dr. Cates, the last thing she wanted to hear were warnings about the man's character. She'd rather find out such things for herself than listen to gossip.

"I'll keep that in mind. See you later, Marti."

At the back of the lodge, in Marshall's airy office, Ruthann sipped leisurely at her latte while Marshall playfully tap-danced around her chair.

"Have you lost your mind, doc?" she asked with a laugh. "First you surprise me with a cup of coffee that cost more than my wristwatch and now you're trying to imitate Fred Astaire. What else do you have planned for today?"

Laughing, he grabbed her swivel chair and spun her in a wild circle that had her yelling for him to stop.

"How about a date with the heiress? That's what I have planned."

She planted her feet on the hardwood floor and stared at his smug face. "Oh. So that's what this display of joy is all about. You've proved me wrong and talked the mystery beauty into a date. I should have guessed. How did you do it?"

Still smiling, he sauntered over to his desk and took a seat in his plush leather chair. "Frankly, Ruthie, I don't have a clue. I ran into her at the coffee shop and—" He stopped and held up a hand. "Wait a minute, I'd better tell you about last night first. I saw her, the mystery beauty, dining at the Gallatin Room last night."

Ruthann lowered her coffee and frowned at him. "It's a good thing we don't have any patients waiting this morning, cause I'd like to hear what you were doing having dinner in the Gallatin Room. You have so much money that you've decided to start throwing it away?"

His expression suddenly sheepish, Marshall shrugged. "I took Lizbeth out to dinner."

Ruthann groaned out loud. "Oh, Lord, Marshall, what were you thinking? She's nothing but a big flirt."

He batted a dismissive hand at her. "Never mind Lizbeth. I'm not serious about her."

Ruthann's expression turned incredulous. "And you are serious about the mystery woman?"

Marshall chuckled at his nurse's question. "Ruthie, you know me, I don't have plans to get serious about any woman. Why should I? I'm having too much fun."

She smirked. "Why indeed? Have you ever thought of children? Of someone to spend your golden days with?"

Marshall's barked laugh said he was worried about Ruthann's sanity. "Just how old do you think I am, Ruthie? I've got years ahead of me before I think about anything like a family. Right now I've got mountains to climb."

She leveled a thoughtful look at him. "And what are you going to find when you reach the top?"

Tilting the plush chair to a reclining position, he linked his hands at the back of his neck and let out a smug sigh. "The satisfaction of getting there. That's what I'll find."

"Satisfaction, huh? Well, you go on climbing, doc. I'd rather have two loving arms around me."

Chapter Four

Later that evening, before it was time to meet Marshall, Mia sat on the bed in her cabin and slowly sifted through the stack of photos in her hand. She wasn't at all sure why she'd packed the snapshots when she'd left Colorado.

Maybe she'd brought them along as a reminder of all she'd left behind. The photos were the only images she had of herself with her birth mother. They'd been taken during Mia's twenty-sixth birthday party, which had been held at Janelle's lavish home.

A frown tugged at the corners of her mouth. She still couldn't think of the mansion in

Denver as her home. But for nearly two years Mia had lived there with her birth mother. During that time she'd tried to fit into Janelle's rich social life and accustom herself to the role of an heiress. All of which had been a drastic change for the young woman who until then had been struggling to work her way through school.

With a sigh, Mia stared at the snapshot in front of her. No one could mistake the identity of the tall woman with her arm draped affectionately around Mia's shoulders. She was almost the mirror image of Mia, only older. One minute Mia had been a young woman in nursing school who longed for the safe and secure home she'd had when her father had still been alive and working their potato farm, a young woman on a long and seemingly fruitless search for her birth mother. The next minute she'd not only found Janelle Josephson but she also discovered the woman was unbelievably rich. After that, Mia and her adopted mother's life had taken a drastic turn.

For years Mia had hunted her birth mother and for just as many years Nina had tried to dissuade her from the search, insisting that Mia's birth mother didn't want to be found. But

Mia had felt driven to find the woman who'd signed her baby girl over to a stranger.

In the end, both Janelle and Mia had been shocked at the occurrences that had separated mother and daughter. Controlling parents had led a teenage Janelle to believe her baby was stillborn. She'd had no idea that her daughter was alive and searching for her. As for Mia, it was difficult for her to absorb the fact that she had a wealthy mother, one who seemingly loved her and was only too happy to lavish her with all the treasures and resources that money could buy.

What happens when a person goes from poverty to riches? Mia was a good example of that age-old question. Suddenly she could have any material thing she wanted, but none of it had made her happy.

For a moment the turmoil in Mia's heart brought a stinging mist to her eyes. But then she determinedly pressed her lips together and shoved the photos in the nightstand drawer.

Right now she needed to put her troubled reflections away and put on the cheeriest face she could muster. It was almost time for her to walk down to the lodge and meet Dr. Cates. And she wanted to give the jovial, flirty doctor the impression that she was just as carefree and happy as he.

Minutes later, Mia walked into the lounge and spotted her date sitting on the end of a plush leather couch. He was focusing intently on the BlackBerry in his hand and for a brief moment Mia paused to study his sexy image.

Even after she'd become an heiress, she'd never dreamed a man of his stature would show interest in her. But she realized that if the doctor knew the real truth of her past, he wouldn't be sitting here waiting to have an evening with her.

Tonight, however, she wasn't going to dwell on that, she wanted to have fun and see if she could remember how to enjoy herself on a simple date.

Mia was walking across the lounge and had almost reached the couch where he was sitting, when he happened to look up and spot her approach.

The quick leap of her heart surprised her. For so long now she'd felt numb. Incapable of feeling anything.

Smiling broadly, he rose to his feet and shoved the BlackBerry into the pocket of his blue jeans. As she walked toward him, he quickly closed the last few steps separating them.

"Hello, Ms. Smith," he said warmly.

His voice was just rough enough to be sexy and she wondered what it would sound like if he were to whisper in her ear.

Smiling in return, she thrust her hand toward his. "Please make it Mia. Calling each other Ms. and Dr. over a burger would be a little ridiculous, don't you think?"

"And shaking hands with a beautiful woman is more than ridiculous for me," he said. And before she could guess his intentions, he leaned forward and placed a gentle kiss on her cheek. "There. That's a much better greeting, don't you think?"

His dancing brown eyes held hers, and Mia realized she was far too charmed to scold him for being forward. The skin along her cheekbone tingled where his lips had touched her and she was getting that breathless feeling all over again.

Deliberately avoiding his pointed question, she said, "I hope you haven't been waiting long."

"Not more than five minutes," he answered. "Are you ready to go? Or would you like to have a drink at the bar before we leave the lodge?"

"Actually, I'm hungry. Let's save the drink for another time." If there was another time, she reminded herself. If Marti's opinion of this man was correct, he'd probably have a different woman on his arm tomorrow night.

"Great," he said. "Let's go. My Jeep is waiting outside the lodge."

Figuring his "jeep" would be one of those plush SUV's that could comfortably haul seven, she was surprised to find his vehicle was one of those compact two-seaters built high off the ground and generally used to traverse rough terrain.

After helping her negotiate the lofty step up, Marshall skirted the hood and quickly slid beneath the wheel. While he buckled his seat belt and started the engine, Mia glanced around the small interior. Behind them, a small bench seat was loaded down with a canvas backpack and a pair of boots caked with mud. An assortment of empty bottles that had one time held water and sports drinks lay on the floorboard below. In front, a small crate of CD's was wedged between the console and the dash. Hanging from the rearview mirror was a small dream catcher made of black and white feathers.

"I promise I cleaned the dog hair from your seat before I drove over here to the lodge. The rest of the mess I hope you'll forgive. I get busy doing things I enjoy and put off all the tasks I hate."

Actually she was relieved that he hadn't shown up in some sleek, spotless luxury car. This vehicle made him seem far more human and closer to the lifestyle Mia had been accustomed to before Janelle had taken her in and presented her with a treasure trove of riches.

"It's fine," she assured him as she adjusted the seat belt across her lap. "You say you have a dog?"

He shoved the floor shift into Reverse and backed out of the parking slot. "A blue heeler named Leroy. He's spoiled worse than I am."

Mia smiled faintly as she glanced over at him. "I take it you spoiled him, but who spoiled you?"

He grinned that sexy grin of his and Mia was suddenly reminded of their close quarters. If she were so minded, she could easily reach over and curl her hand over his forearm.

"My mother insists she ruined all of her boys. Much to Dad's dismay," he added with a chuckle.

Interest peaked her brows. "You have brothers?"

"Three. Mitchell. He's thirty. And the twins, Matthew and Marlon, are twenty-one."

Three brothers and a complete set of parents, Mia couldn't imagine having a more wonderful family. "Where do you fit in among the bunch?"

"I'm thirty-four, the oldest of the Cates brood. My parents live north of town, not too far out. Maybe you'd like to meet them before you leave?"

Meet his parents? No. She didn't think so. Making too many memories here might make it that much harder to leave. And she would have to leave soon, she reminded herself. She couldn't continue to hide from Janelle much longer.

"Maybe," she answered.

By now they were leaving the resort area and the Jeep was heading south on Thunder Canyon Road. Ahead of them on the far horizon, the sun was sinking, spreading a golden-pink glow over the mountain basin.

"I guess all the hoopla over the Queen of Hearts mine is what drew you to this area? Or did you choose to stay at Thunder Canyon Resort for other reasons?"

The only reason she'd ended up in Thunder Canyon was because she'd gotten lost on her way out of Bozeman. Originally she'd been intending to travel all the way into Canada. But

Marshall Cates didn't need to know the story of her life.

"I thought it would be beautiful and peaceful. And when I saw your little town with its Old West storefronts and flavor, I was enchanted. I didn't know anything about gold being found in Thunder Canyon until I'd been here a few days. From what I hear, the discovery has turned the place upside down."

With a wry twist to his lips, he nodded. "I never realized money could make people go so crazy. People who've been friends around here for years are now fighting over choice lots in town. Everyone wants to get their hands on a piece of the fortune that's coming in from the crush of tourists."

I never realized money could make people go so crazy, thought Mia.

Marshall didn't know it, but he could have spoken those very words about her. For a while money had slanted her every thought and controlled every choice she'd made. Now having the stuff was more like a dirty little secret that she couldn't hide or discard.

Stifling a sigh, she said, "Well, I've overheard several women in the Clip 'N' Curl beauty salon talking about all the changes that have come to this area. Some of them like the opportunities the gold find has brought about. Others seem pretty resentful of all the traffic as well as all the strangers clomping up and down the sidewalks of their little town. How do you feel?"

Shrugging, he glanced at her and grinned. "Personally, I don't understand these people that want to hang on to the past. Hell, before the gold rush, lots of folks around here were hurting for jobs and an income of any kind. Now most of them are doing better than anyone ever thought possible, including me. And frankly, I don't see anything wrong with a man wanting to do better for himself."

No, Mia thought, doing better for oneself was hardly a crime. Unless somewhere along the way the rush for riches harmed innocent people. The way Mia's desperate need for financial security had ultimately harmed her dear adopted mother.

"I guess it's all in the way a person sees things," she murmured thoughtfully.

He tossed her another grin. "That was put very diplomatically, Mia. Maybe you should referee some of Thunder Canyon's town hall meetings," he added teasingly. "There's been so much feuding going on that the police have to hang close just in case a fight breaks out."

"No, thank you. I'm not into politics, local or otherwise."

She'd hardly gotten the words out of her mouth when the outskirts of town appeared in the distance. In a few short minutes they were passing the town's outdoor ice rink, now a quiet arena in the summer heat; then just around the corner was the Wander-On Inn, a stately old hotel that had originally been built and operated by Lily Divine, Thunder Canyon's own lady of ill repute.

As Mia studied the landmark, Marshall said, "Lily Divine first built that old hotel. If you've read anything about Thunder Canyon's history, you probably haven't forgotten her name. She's been called everything from a wicked madam to a noble suffragette. Her great-great-granddaughter Lisa Douglas owns the Queen of Hearts mine." He shook his head as if that fact was still hard to believe. "Now there's a rags-to-riches story. A couple of years ago, the woman was as poor as dirt and then she finds out she's the owner of a lucrative gold mine. I can't imagine how that sudden catapult must have felt."

Mia could have told Marshall exactly how finding sudden fortune felt. One day she'd been wondering if she could make two meals out of a package of wieners and the next she was eating steak from a gold-rimmed plate. The drastic change in her life had sent her emotions spinning in all directions.

Careful to keep her expression smooth, she asked, "This Lisa…is she happy now?"

Something in her voice pulled Marshall's glance over to her. She looked wistful, even hopeful, and Marshall could only wonder why she would be so interested in the outcome of a person who was a total stranger to her.

"I suppose so. She married one of the Douglases, a family that probably owns half the valley. In fact, his old man built the resort where you're staying. She'll never want for anything again."

Her lips pursed and then her gaze dropped to her lap and a curtain of black hair swung forward to hide her pained expression. "You can't be sure of that," she said quietly. "People die—things change."

"Yeah. But she'll always have the money."

Her head jerked up and she glared at him as though he'd just uttered a blasphemy. "What does that mean? You think money can take the place of a loved one? Well, it can't!"

Her voice was quivering with outrage and Marshall was befuddled as to why she'd reacted so strongly to his comment. With his right hand he reached over and gently touched her forearm. "Whoa, Mia. Don't get so bent out of shape. I just meant that she'd always have financial security. I like money just as much as the next guy, but my loved ones mean more to me than anything—even a gold mine, if I had one."

His gaze left the road long enough to see her release a long breath and her pretty features twist with regret.

"I—I'm sorry, Marshall. Having money has made me too touchy, I guess. But people say insensitive things, especially when they don't understand that we have problems, too."

He wanted to ask her what sort of problems she was talking about, but he could see she was hardly in the mood. Besides, he sensed the woman needed joy and laughter in her life and that was the very thing he wanted to give her.

"You're right, Mia. People are too quick to judge. But let's not have a philosophical discussion about human nature right now. I want to have fun with you tonight. Okay?"

She nodded jerkily and he was relieved to see a faint smile cross her face.

"Sure," she said. "I didn't mean to suddenly get so serious on you. Let's start over, shall we?"

Marshall gave her a broad smile. "Okay, we'll start over. Good evening, Mia. What would you like to eat tonight?"

"Burgers and fries. I'm sure you advise your patients not to eat such things, but maybe you can forget about the fat and calories for one night."

Glad to see she was going to follow his suggestion and lighten up, he chuckled. "Believe me, Mia, doctors don't always practice what they preach. Burgers and fries sound great to me."

At the next intersection, he made a right onto South Main. As they passed the town square with its shade trees and park benches, he said, "There's a little place right down here where I used to eat in all the time when I worked at Thunder Canyon General. They serve plain home-cooked meals and the burgers are great. You can even have a buffalo burger if you'd like."

Her nose wrinkled playfully. "I'm afraid I'm not quite that adventurous. I think I'll stick to plain ole beef."

Moments later Marshall parked the Jeep near a small bar and grill. As they walked down the rough board sidewalk, Mia noticed the front of this particular building was made to look like an

Old West saloon, complete with swinging doors.

As they entered the dim interior, she could feel Marshall's hand flatten against the small of her back. And though she'd expected his touch to feel warm and strong, she'd not expected the wild zings of awareness spreading through her body.

Bending his head down to hers, he spoke close to her ear in order to be heard above the country music blaring from the jukebox in the far corner.

"We seat ourselves here at the Rusty Spur," he said. "How about a table over by the wall?"

"Fine with me," she answered.

Tonight the bar and grill appeared to be the popular place to be. Most of the round wooden tables and chairs were filled with diners and beer drinkers. Everyone was dressed casually and seemed to be laughing and talking and generally having a good time. Quite a contrast from the elegant Gallatin Room, she thought wryly.

As soon as Marshall helped her into a chair and took his own seat, a fresh-faced young waitress with a blond ponytail stopped at the side of their table to take their orders.

When Mia requested a soda to go with her

food, Marshall said, "They serve beer here that's made at a nearby brewery. It's really good. Wouldn't you like to try one?"

Mia tried not to outwardly stiffen at his suggestion. She wasn't a prude, but after seeing Nina become dependant on alcohol she preferred to limit herself.

With a shake of her head, she said, "No. Soda is fine. But you please go ahead."

While Marshall gave the waitress their order, Mia looked around the L-shaped room. The ceiling was low and crisscrossed with dark wooden beams; the walls were made of tongue and groove painted a pale green. Not far from the swinging door entrance, a long bar, also fashioned from dark wood, ran for several feet. Swiveling stools with low backs of carved wooden spokes served as chairs; at the moment they were all filled with customers.

As the waitress finished scribbling onto her pad and hurried away, Mia turned her attention back to him.

"This seems to be a popular place. You say you used to eat here when you worked at Thunder Canyon General. You worked at the hospital before you took the job at the resort?"

He nodded. "I went to work there right after I finished my internship."

Mia thoughtfully studied his handsome face and realized there were more layers to the man than she'd expected to find.

"What sort of medicine did you practice there? The same thing you do at the resort?"

As Mia watched the corners of his mouth curve upward, she could feel her heart flutter like a happy little bird. Which was totally ridiculous. She'd had men smile at her before, even good-looking men. But they'd not made her blood hum with excitement the way that Marshall did.

"Mostly E.R. work."

"Did you like doing that?"

For a moment he was thoughtful, as though he'd never stopped to ask himself that question. "I suppose. There was always something different going on."

Easing back in her chair, she said knowingly, "But you like your job at the resort better."

His laugh was a mixture of amusement and disbelief. "Of course. Why wouldn't I? It's a cushy job. On most days I only see a handful of patients. I'm provided with a great nurse and the resort pays the astronomical cost of medical liability for me."

The waitress arrived with their drinks. After Mia had taken a long sip of her soda she said,

"Is that what you went to medical school for? To get a job like you have at the resort? Or did you become a doctor so you could help people?"

Laughing lowly, he shook a playful finger at her. "Now, now, Ms. Smith. We weren't going to have philosophical discussions, tonight. Remember?"

Blushing faintly, she smiled. "Okay. I won't dig at that anymore. So tell me about your siblings. Do you get along with them?"

"Sure. We're all good buddies. 'Course, with Mitchell and I being closer in age, that made us a little tighter, I suppose. We love our twin brothers, too, but growing up they were just a little too young to do much with us."

"Any of them like sports as much as you?"

"Kind of, the twins are into baseball and football, sports of that sort. But Mitchell is more of a brain than an athlete. I couldn't pay him to climb a mountain with me."

"I don't blame him," Mia said. "It's dangerous stuff."

"Not if you know what you're doing." He leaned toward her, his dark brown eyes twinkling in a way that warmed her blood even more. "I could teach you."

Mia laughed and as she did she realized this

was the first time since her mother had died that she'd felt this good. Before she realized what she was doing, she reached over and squeezed his hand with her fingers.

"You must be an optimist, Marshall, if you think you can teach me to climb a mountain. I'm too awkward and certainly not strong enough."

His thumb reached out and curved over hers. The touch was ridiculously intimate, but although Mia told herself to pull away, her body wouldn't obey her brain's instructions. His touch made her feel secure, even wanted. Something she hadn't felt in a long time.

"You hiked all the way up to the bluff on Hawk's Home. That's a pretty stiff climb."

His compliment put a warm blush on her cheeks. "Thank you for the confidence. But that's hiking. That's not what you do with the pulleys and ropes and such."

"I can teach you all that. In baby steps, of course."

The grin on his face deepened, showcasing his dimples. It was hard for Mia to concentrate on their conversation; her senses were spinning, her mind conjuring up all sorts of sexual images.

"I—don't know. Maybe before I leave you can take me on a baby climb."

Surprise and then pleasure swept across his face. "I'd like that, Mia. You'd be the first woman to go climbing with me."

She shot him a skeptical look. "You don't really expect me to believe that, do you?"

"Why not? Most of the women I've dated don't like to do that much outdoor strenuous stuff. A bicycle ride maybe. But not mountain climbing."

For some reason, Mia didn't want to be compared to his other dates. Nor did she want to think of him as a playboy or herself as just one of many women who'd sat across a table from him and held his hand.

Easing her fingers away from his, she said, "Shows you how much sense I have."

The grin on his lips eased to a pleased curve. "No, it means you're unique. Just like I imagined you'd be."

She was unique, all right, Mia thought wryly. If he looked for a hundred years, he wouldn't find another woman who'd turned her back on the loving mother who raised her. He wouldn't find another woman stupid enough to think that financial security would fix all the ills in her life.

Yes, Mia was unique, all right, but in all the

wrong ways. Hopefully, Marshall Cates wouldn't discover any of those terrible things about her until long after she'd left Thunder Canyon.

Chapter Five

Before Mia and Marshall left the Rusty Spur, he insisted that the two of them needed dessert and asked the waitress to get them a container of Golden Nugget to go.

Later, after Marshall had paid for the meal and the two of them had left the building, she looked suspiciously at the brown paper sack in his hand.

"What is that—did you call it Golden Nugget?"

His grin mischievous, he helped her into the Jeep. "I did. They conjured up this stuff shortly after the gold strike. You'll find out what it is when we get to where we're going to eat it."

"A man of mystery," she said teasingly. "Well, I suppose I'll just have to wait for this surprise dessert."

Once he'd pulled away from the bar and grill, he turned the vehicle toward North Main. While he negotiated the busy narrow streets, Mia realized she hadn't felt this warm and mellow in a long time. Like their meal, their conversation had been simple and comfortable. She was enjoying being with the man far more than she had expected.

To Mia's surprise, Marshall drove them straight to Thunder Canyon Road and stopped the Jeep in the large graveled parking lot of the ice rink.

"What are we doing at an outdoor ice rink in August?"

Marshall's chuckle was suggestive enough to lift her brows. "We're going to eat our dessert, what else?" he asked.

Picking up the brown paper bag, he left the vehicle and came around to help her down to the ground. As Mia placed her hand in his she felt a rush of naughty excitement. After nearly three years of avoiding men altogether, being out with a man as sexy and sensual as Marshall was like having a plateful of cherry pie after a long stretch of dieting. Sinful, but delicious.

Once she was standing on the ground, he slipped his free arm around the back of her waist and guided her toward the rink, which was surrounded by a chain-link fence and dimly lit by one lone lamp standing near a small building that was used as a warming room. The gate was unlocked and once they were inside the compound they walked over to one of the wooden benches looking out over the rink.

A huge cottonwood tree shaded the seat while overhead the fluttering leaves were making soft music in the evening breeze. In the far distance, the mountains surrounding Thunder Canyon Resort loomed like majestic sentinels robed in deep greens and purples. Mia sighed with pleasure as she sank onto the bench.

"It's pretty here. I'll bet it's really nice when the rink is frozen over and skaters are whirling about. Do you skate?" she asked.

"Sure do. Our parents taught all of us boys how to skate long before we ever went to kindergarten." He smiled fondly out at the now empty rink. "I've had some really fun times here. Even when I cracked my wrist."

He began to open the paper bag and pull out a quart-sized paper carton. When he pulled off the lid she could see it held something that looked like ice cream.

"Oh. A cracked wrist doesn't sound like fun to me."

He handed her one of the two plastic spoons.

"Several of us skaters had made a dandy whip and I was getting a heck of a ride out on the tail end. It was a blast until the g-force finally got me and I flew completely off the ice and crashed into a bench like the one we're sitting on. My wrist was in a cast for six weeks."

Mia gave him a knowing smile. "Sounds like you were a little daredevil. I'll bet you gave your mother plenty of gray hairs."

"Probably more than a few," he admitted with a wry smile. "But my parents always encouraged us to be independent and adventurous. I think it stuck on me the most."

He thrust the container toward her. "Dig in. I can't eat all this by myself."

Mia followed his example and spooned up a bite. As the ice cream melted on her tongue, she closed her eyes and savored the taste. "Mmm. You were right. This is scrumptious."

"See, the streaks of caramel are supposed to represent veins of ore and the chunks of almonds are the gold nuggets. This is definitely one good thing that came out of the Queen of Hearts striking it rich. Next to you, that is," he added with a wink.

Mia understood his words were just playful flirting, but she also considered how nice it would be—and more than flattering—for a man like him to look at her in a serious way. When her father had still been alive and her life had been fairly secure, she'd been smart enough to know that she'd never belong to the elite of the world. She didn't dream of marrying a prince or even a doctor or a lawyer. She'd always pictured herself with a farmer or, at the very most, a man who made his living working outdoors, like Lance, who'd worked as a Colorado forest ranger.

But after a tumultuous year of dating, Lance had walked away from her, she thought grimly. He'd tired of her obsessive search for her birth mother, then later he'd hated the woman she'd changed into after finding Janelle and her inheritance.

Trying to shake away that dismal thought, she lifted her gaze to Marshall and gave him a lopsided smile. "You need to remember that Golden Nugget is a permanent fixture here in Thunder Canyon. I'm not."

His spoon paused in midair as the corners of

his mouth turned downward in an exaggerated frown. "You're not leaving soon, are you?"

This past week Mia had been telling herself that it was time to go, time to get back to reality and finally make a few painful decisions concerning her relationship with Janelle. But then she'd met Marshall on the mountain and now she was foolishly looking for any reason to stay at the resort a few days longer.

Dropping her gaze to the ice-cream container wedged between their thighs, she murmured, "I don't suppose it's necessary for me to leave in the next few days. But I—really should."

The last word had hardly died on her lips when his forefinger slid beneath her chin and lifted her face up to his. The serious look she saw on his handsomely carved features jolted her; her heart pounded heavily.

"We're just now getting to know each other, Mia. I really would like you to stay longer."

His gravelly voice was a soft purr and the sound tugged at every feminine particle inside of her. "I—uh—I'll think about it."

Suddenly his head was bending toward hers and the whispered words that passed his lips skittered a warning down her spine.

"Maybe you should think about this."

Mia wasn't totally naive. She knew what was coming and knew she should jump from the bench and put a respectable distance between herself and the handsome doctor. But longing and even a bit of curiosity held her motionless as his lips descended onto hers.

Cool and sweet from the ice cream, his hard lips moved gently, coaxingly over hers. Mia's senses quickly began to tilt. In search of an anchor, her hands reached for his shoulders and she gripped the muscles as the lazy foray of his kiss went on and on.

By the time he finally lifted his head, Mia was breathless and her face was burning.

"A man isn't supposed to kiss a woman like that on their first date," she said as primly as she could, while inside she was quaking, shocked that she could feel such connection from a single kiss.

A crooked grin spread across his face and even in the semidarkness she could see that his brown eyes were shining as though he'd just conquered a dragon and laid it at her feet.

"Well, I was pretending that this was our second date. Forgive me if I was too forward."

She swallowed as emotions tangled into a ball in her throat. "You were. But that's my fault. I should have stopped you in the first place."

Before he could make any reply, she jumped from the bench and began walking around the edge of the rink. The deep reaction she'd felt to Marshall's kiss had left her almost frantic and she told herself she should have never agreed to this date in the first place. It was clear that nothing meaningful could ever happen between them. Being with him was asking for trouble.

Her mind was spinning with all sorts of agonizing thoughts when his hand came down on her shoulder and stopped her forward motion.

"Mia, wait. Don't be angry."

Quickly, she turned to face him and when she spoke Marshall was surprised to hear her voice was almost contrite. As though she were apologizing for kissing him. The idea stunned him.

"I'm not angry at you, Marshall. I—"

Before she could react, he wrapped his arms around her and pulled her close against him. "You're a beautiful woman, Mia. I've wanted to kiss you ever since I met you. There's nothing wrong in what just happened between us."

Even though it had been more like an earthquake than a kiss, Marshall thought. His head was still reeling, but he was wise enough to know that he had to play down the whole thing.

She was already trying to run from him and he couldn't let that happen. One way or the other he was going to make her his woman—at least for a while.

Her fingers fluttered against his chest while farther down her thighs were brushing against his. Desire surged through him like a prairie wildfire.

"Marshall, I'm just a tourist. The most we can ever be is friends. And friends don't touch each other like this."

She started to push him away, but he held her for a moment longer. "You and I are going to be more than friends, little darlin'. You might as well take my word on that."

Frowning, she stepped out of the circle of his arms and marched back in the direction of where they'd been sitting. Marshall tempered his long strides to match hers.

"Are you this—this arrogant and cocky and overly confident with your other dates?" she demanded.

He laughed. "I don't know. My other dates have never stirred me up like this."

She shot him a glare. "Then you'd better give yourself a pill to get unstirred, doc. Because I have no intention of becoming one of your many lovers!"

By now they were back at the gate that would lead them to the parked Jeep. As her hand reached to open the latch, Marshall caught it with his.

"Whoa now, Ms. Smith. Somewhere along the way things have gotten way out of hand. I'd like to know where this 'many' came from?" he asked crossly. "How would you know how many women I've bedded?"

Her lips pressed tightly together, then she deliberately turned her head away from him. "I shouldn't have said that. I'm sorry. It's none of my business anyway."

More frustrated than he could ever remember being, Marshall raked a hand through his hair and blew out a weary breath. "Okay. I'm sorry, too. I shouldn't have thrown that taunt at you. I just—well—I like you, Mia. I really like you." His voice was a low, gentle murmur as he dared to step closer. "And I do want us to be more than friends. There's nothing wrong in being honest with you, is there?"

Her head turned back to his and he was disappointed to see that her expression was carefully guarded, as though she didn't trust him enough to allow him to see what she was actually feeling and thinking. It wasn't the first time he'd noticed the curtain she pulled across her features and he suddenly vowed to himself that he was going to learn what was behind those beautiful eyes, no matter how long it took or how painstaking the effort.

"No. I do appreciate your being up-front with me," she said finally. "I'm just trying to tell you that I'm not in the market for a brief affair."

His fingertips made gentle circles on the back of her hand. "Why? Do you have a boyfriend or fiancé waiting for you back in Denver?"

Her lips parted and she hesitated for a split second before she replied, "No. There's no significant man in my life."

Marshall didn't realize how much her answer meant to him until she said it. Relief poured through him like a warm spring rain.

"Look, Mia, I'm not asking you to have an affair with me. I'm just asking you to spend time with me and see where it takes us. That's all." Taking her hand between his, he gave her a pleading grin. "I think we can have fun together, Mia. And I have a feeling you could use a little of that."

A few stilted moments passed before she let out a soft sigh and the stiffness in her body melted away.

With a halfhearted smile, she said, "I'm

sorry, Marshall. I shouldn't have overreacted the way I did."

"Forget it. I'm just as guilty." His fingertips tenderly touched her cheek. "What do you say we go finish the ice cream?"

Her quiet laugh warmed his heart.

"It's probably melted by now."

Draping his arm around her shoulders, Marshall turned her back toward the ice rink. "Then we'll drink it."

Two days later, Marshall's Thursday turned out to be a busy day at the infirmary. He'd tended everything from strained knees to poison ivy to bee stings. However, the last patient he examined didn't have the usual external problems he normally encountered. The middle-aged woman he was treating complained of stomach complications. She was dressed in casual but expensive clothes and her jewelry shouted that her bank account was overflowing. Yet Marshall didn't miss the fact that her ring finger was conspicuously empty.

"I really think it's just a virus, doctor. If you could just give me something for the pain—my stomach feels like it's clenching into a tight ball."

Stepping back from his patient, Marshall

studied her face. She'd obviously had a face-lift at some point. The job wasn't a bad one, but as a doctor he could easily pick up on the telltale tightened skin. Her light blond hair had been manufactured at a beauty salon, probably to cover the gray that was beginning to frost her temples. Yet on the whole she was an attractive woman, or would be, he decided, if her eyes weren't filled with such sadness.

Is that why you went to medical school? To get a cushy job? Or did you become a doctor so you could help people?

Mia's pointed questions suddenly hit him like a brick. Normally, he wouldn't have taken the extra time to dig into this patient's problem. In the past Marshall would have simply written her a prescription to relieve her symptoms and sent her on her way. She obviously needed more help than he could give her. But now, with Mia gnawing at his conscience he felt compelled to do more for this woman.

"Ms. Phillips, I have my doubts that your stomach problem is a virus. Something like that usually lasts no longer than a couple of days and you tell me this problem has been going on for two or three weeks."

She nodded. "That's right. It started while I was still home, but I ignored it. I thought once

I got here at the resort I'd feel better. You know, getting out and away from…things always makes a person forget their aches and pains."

Thoughtfully, he placed the clipboard he was holding on the edge of a cabinet counter. "Do you have a family, Ms. Phillips?"

A nervous smile played upon her carefully lined lips. "Call me, Doris, doctor. And yes, I have…a daughter. She's grown now and just married this past spring."

"That's nice. And what about your husband?"

She suddenly looked away from him and her fingers fiddled nervously with the crease of her slacks. "I'm not married anymore. We're divorced. He—uh—found someone else."

"Oh. I'm sorry. Guess that's been hard on you."

Her short laugh was brittle. "Twenty years of marriage down the drain. Yes, it's been a little worse than hard. Now my daughter is gone from the house and—and the place is really empty. I decided to come here to the resort to be around people and hopefully make new friends."

Marshall gave her shoulder an encouraging pat. "It's good that you're trying to change your life, Doris, and things will get better. In the meantime, I'm going to give you a prescription that will help ease your stomach. I have an idea that all the stress you've been through is causing the problem and I want to give you this anti-anxiety medication." He pulled a small pad from his lab coat pocket and began to scribble instructions for the pharmacist. "But I want you to come see me again before you leave. If this doesn't help, we'll take a closer look, okay?"

A bright look of relief and gratitude suddenly lit the woman's face. "Yes, doctor. Thank you so much."

Marshall left the examining room with a warm feeling of accomplishment and was still smiling when he met Ruthann at the end of the hallway.

"What's the grin all about?" the nurse asked. "Happy that you've finished the last patient for the day?"

Frowning, he thrust Doris Phillips's chart at her. "Put this away, will you? And no, I'm smiling because I think I just made someone actually feel better."

Rising on her tiptoes, Ruthann placed her palm on his forehead. "Yeah, you're a little flush. One of the patients must have passed a bug to you."

The frown on his face deepened. "Quit it,

will you? I am a doctor, you know. My job is to make people feel better."

He pushed her hand away and stalked toward his office. Ruthann hurried after him. "I was only teasing, doc," she said as he took a seat at his desk. "What's with you, anyway?"

Picking up a pen, he tapped the end against the blotter on his desk as he regarded his concerned nurse. "Nothing is wrong, Ruthie. Aren't I supposed to enjoy my job?"

"Well, yes. But I never remember you— well, you mostly get to the point and send the patients on their way. You were in there so long with Ms. Phillips I was beginning to think she'd attacked you or something."

Was that how Ruthann saw him? Effective but without compassion? Marshall realized he didn't care for that image. But then he had no one but himself to blame.

"The woman has stomach problems and I was trying to get to the root of the matter. She thought she'd picked up a virus but the real germ she's dealing with is an ex-husband."

"Oh. You got that out of her?"

It had been easy, Marshall realized, to get his patient to open up. So why wasn't it easy with Mia Smith? After their date last night, he'd realized that she truly was a mystery woman.

She didn't talk about her family or her past and the shadows that he sometimes noticed clouding her eyes meant that whatever troubles life had thrown her way were still haunting her. But what were they and why did he feel this need to help her?

Seeing that this new, more compassionate side of him was putting a look of real concern on Ruthann's face, he laughed and gave her one of his usual winks.

"Ruthie, I haven't lost my touch with women yet."

Seeing him back to his normal self, Ruthie rolled her eyes with amusement. "And I'm pretty certain you never will." She walked over to a door that would take her into another room where hundreds of charts, most of them from one-time patients, were stored. "Ready to call it an evening? Dr. Baxter should be here any minute."

Dr. Baxter was the doctor who worked evenings and remained on call all night long. The man had much less to do than Marshall, but Grant insisted that medical personnel be available to the guests twenty-four hours a day—just one of the added conveniences that set Thunder Canyon Resort apart from the competition.

"Go ahead, Ruthie, I think I'll stop by the lounge and have a drink before I head home."

Her expression suddenly turned thoughtful as she walked over to his desk. "I hope you're not stopping by to see Lizbeth Stanton. That girl doesn't need any encouragement. She has her eye on you and any man that could give her a home on easy street."

Marshall dismissed Ruthann's remark by batting a hand through the air. "You're being a little too harsh on the woman, Ruthie. She's really not all that bad. She just needs to grow up a little and get her head on straight."

"Well, just as long as you're not the one doing the straightening," Ruthann said.

Laughing, Marshall turned off the banker's lamp on his desk, then rose to his feet and pulled off his lab coat. "Ruthie, I can't go around fixing all my girlfriends. Now," he said, curling an affectionate arm around her shoulders, "how would you like to go to dinner with me at the Gallatin Room some night soon?"

Ruthann practically gaped at him. "Me? With you? At the Gallatin Room?" Before Marshall could answer, she let out a loud laugh, then patted his arm in a motherly way. "I couldn't step foot in that place. Not with the clothes in my closet. But thank you for the gesture, Marshall. It's sweet of you." Leaving his side, she opened the door to the chart room. After she stepped inside, she stuck her head around the door and added, "Listen, doc, that mystery heiress you were so enchanted with the other day is the kind you need to be taking to the Gallatin Room. Why don't you ask her?"

Because something told him that Mia needed more than glitz and glamour and a meal at a ritzy restaurant.

Thankfully, Ruthann didn't expect any sort of answer from him and Marshall didn't give her one. Instead, he quickly hung his lab coat on a nearby hall tree and told his nurse goodbye for the day.

A few minutes later, Marshall entered the lounge. For an early weekday evening, the place was unusually full of guests. But he didn't pay much attention to the people relaxing on the tucked leather couches and armchairs covered in spotted cowhide. Instead, he made his way straight to the bar where Lizbeth was busily doling out mixed drinks to a group of barely legal young men.

Marshall slung his leg over a stool at the end of the bar and waited for her to finish placing a tray of drinks in front of the lively group.

"Hey, what does it take for a guy to get any

service around here?" he called when she finally turned in his direction.

Smiling with apparent pleasure at seeing him, Lizbeth waved and hurried to his end of the polished bar. "Doctor, all you have to do to get a woman's attention is just throw her a grin."

Not where Mia Smith was concerned, he thought. She seemed immune to those things that normally charmed women. Looking at Lizbeth, he inclined his head toward the boisterous group of men at the other end of the bar. "You've got me confused with those young guys."

Resting her forearms on the bar, Lizbeth leaned slightly toward him and lowered her voice so that only he could hear her words. "They just think they know how to flirt with a woman, but they're still wet behind the ears. Unlike you, Dr. Cates."

Any other time Marshall would have laughed at Lizbeth's flirtatious remark, but this evening it only made him feel old and even a bit shallow. It was a hell of a thing when a man was more noted for being a playboy with the women than a doctor to the sick.

"Give me a beer, Lizbeth. Something strong and cold."

"Sure." All business now, she started to push

away from the bar, but at the last moment paused and gave him a thoughtful look. "Just in case you're interested, I saw that *heiress* of yours a few moments ago walk out to the sundeck. She was carrying a book of some sort. You might still find her out there reading. Or maybe she's just pretending to read and really looking at the scenery." To make her point, Lizbeth glanced at the young men she'd just served.

Marshall's head whipped around and his gaze studied the far wall of glass that separated the lounge from the large wooden sundeck. From this vantage point, he could see several people lounging on the bent-willow lawn furniture, but Mia wasn't one of them.

Quickly, he slipped off the stool. "Forget the beer, Lizbeth. I'll catch one later."

As he strode away, he heard the bartender call after him.

"Good luck."

Luck? It was going to take more than that for him to get inside Mia Smith's head and delve into her secrets, he thought as he stepped onto the sundeck. Or was it really her heart that he wanted to unlock and hold in the palm of his hands?

SUSAN FOX

Chapter Six

Marshall was asking himself how a question of that sort had ever gotten into his mind when he spotted her. She was stretched out in a lounger, her long legs crossed at the knees, her shiny black hair lying in one thick, single braid against her shoulder. A book was open on her lap, but her gaze was not on the pages. Instead she was staring straight at him and the tiny smile that suddenly curved her lips hit Marshall smack in the middle of his chest.

If he'd been a smart man he would have turned and run in the opposite direction just as hard and fast as he could. But when it came to the opposite sex, Marshall was as weak as a kid in a candy shop. And Mia Smith was definitely one delectable piece of candy.

Feeling like a man possessed, he walked to her chair and squatted on his heels near the arm so that his face would be level with hers.

"Hello, Mia."

"Hi yourself."

Her voice was soft, sweet and husky. The sound shivered over him and for one fleeting moment he felt like a humble knight kneeling to the princess fair.

"Lizbeth told me I might find you out here. Been reading?" He glanced briefly at the hardback book in her lap, then back to her face. There was a faint hint of color on her cheekbones and lips, but for the most part it was bare of makeup, giving him a hint at the natural beauty he would see if he were to wake and find her head pillowed on his shoulder.

"Trying. But the story is rather slow. And there's a bit too much distraction around the lodge," she added with a pointed smile.

"That's me. A distraction," he jokingly replied while everything inside of him wanted to reach for her hand and bring the back of it to his lips. He wanted to taste the soft skin and watch the reaction on her face.

Folding the book together, she swung her legs over the side of the lounger where he was still crouched. She was so close that the flowery scent of her perfume drifted to his nostrils and the palm of his hand itched to slide up her bare thigh.

"Are you finished with work for the day?" she asked.

He nodded, then with a nervousness that was totally foreign to him, he asked, "Do you have plans for the evening?"

Marshall's question made Mia realize just how unplanned her life was at this moment. Staying here at Thunder Canyon Resort was easy and pleasant. But she was living in limbo and sooner or later she was going to have to step over the dividing line.

A sardonic smile touched her lips. "I don't really have anyone around here to make plans with."

"You have me."

His simple words unsettled her far more than he could ever know and, to cover her discomfiture, she rose to her feet and walked over to a low balustrade that lined the edge of the sundeck.

Slanted rays of the sinking sun painted the distant bluffs and forests a golden green. Below them, guests ambled around the manicured grounds of the resort. As her senses whirled with his blatant comment, Mia carefully kept her gaze on the sights in front of her.

"That is—if you want me."

She hadn't realized he'd walked up behind her until his murmured words were spoken next to her ear. She tried not to shiver as his warm breath danced across the side of her cheek.

"I—uh—enjoyed last night," she admitted. In fact, Mia had lain awake most of the night, reliving the connection she'd felt when Marshall had kissed her. It had been more than a fiery meeting of lips. The kiss had been full of emotions so ripe with longing and sensuality that she'd felt it all the way to her heart. And that scared her.

His body eased next to hers and she felt his warm arm encircling the back of her waist.

"So did I," he said lowly.

Part of her started to melt as his fingertips slid back and forth against her forearm.

She was trying to think of any sensible thing to say when he spoke again.

"And I was wondering before I ever left my office if you'd like to have dinner with me again."

All sorts of skeptical thoughts raced through her head. What could a successful man like him find attractive about her, she asked herself. She was not a raving beauty or a sexy party girl. She wasn't even much of a conversationalist. As far as she was concerned she was totally boring. She was also a fake. How long would it take him to figure her out, she wondered dismally.

"Dinner tonight?"

He nodded and she couldn't mistake the sensual glint in his green-brown eyes. As his gaze traveled slowly over her face, the suggestive sparkle warmed her cheeks.

"Sure. Have you eaten yet?"

If Mia had had any sense at all, she would have lied and told him she'd just stuffed herself at the Grubstake, a fast-food grill located in the lounge. At least that way she'd have an excuse to politely turn him down. But the awful truth was that she didn't want to turn the man down. Being with him was too exciting, too tempting for her lonely heart to pass up.

"No. Before you walked out here I was thinking about grabbing a salad at the Grubstake."

His nose wrinkled with disapproval. "You need more than rabbit food. How about letting me grill you a steak at my place? I'm pretty handy as a chef." A corner of his lips curved up in a modest grin. "An outdoor chef, that is."

She hesitantly studied his face. "At your place?"

The grin on his face deepened, saying she had nothing to fear, and when his fingertips reached out to trace a lazy circle on her cheek, she knew she was lost.

"Yes, my place. I live here on the resort, not far from the lodge. I'd like for you to see it. And while you're there you can meet Leroy. He loves company."

Seeing his home, meeting his dog—did she really want to let herself get closer to this man? Especially when she knew she could never have a meaningful relationship with him.

"I…Marshall…"

As she began to hesitate, he wrapped his arm around hers and led her away from the balustrade toward a set of steps that would take them off the sundeck. "I'm not about to let you say no," he said. "So don't even try."

"Okay, okay," she said, laughing. "But I need to go home and change first."

He glanced pointedly at her denim shorts and pale yellow T-shirt. "Why? You look great to me and I'm the only one who's going to see you. Besides, this is going to be a casual affair."

Knowing she'd already lost, Mia groaned with surrender and allowed him to lead her around to the back of the massive ski lodge to the private parking area where his Jeep was parked.

The drive to his home took less than five minutes on a winding road that spiraled up the mountainside. Spruce and aspen trees grew right to the edge of the road and shaded patches of delicate blue and gold wildflowers nodding in the evening breeze.

Suddenly the road widened and the Jeep leveled onto a wide driveway. Mia leaned forward at the sight of a large log structure with a steep red-metal roof nestled among several pines and cedars.

A graveled walkway lined with large white stones led up to a long, slightly elevated porch made of wooden planks. Ferns and blooming petunias grew in baskets hanging along a roof that was supported by more thick logs. Double doors made of wood and frosted glass served as an entrance to the charming structure.

"Wow, is this the sort of housing all the employees at the resort get?"

His chuckle was almost a little guilty. "No. I'm an exception. When the resort was first being constructed, this house was actually built to rent as a honeymoon suite. But for some reason that was nixed and I ended up getting it for my digs."

She glanced at him curiously as he parked the Jeep in front of the house. "Why? Because you're the resort's doctor?"

His expression a bit sheepish, he answered, "No. Grant Clifton, the manager of the resort, is a good friend of mine. We grew up together and attended the same school. It helps to have friends in high places."

Had it helped her to have a mother in high places? Mia asked herself. She'd be lying to say it hadn't. She was no longer scraping pennies to buy gas for a clunker car to carry her from a ratty apartment to the college campus, or wondering how she was going to find enough in the cabinets to cook a meal for her adoptive mother and herself. But in most ways Janelle's massive wealth had only caused Mia grief and more trouble than she could have possibly imagined. From the moment she'd found Janelle, the woman had smothered her with love and money. By themselves those two things would have been good, but along with the love and money, Janelle had also wanted to hold on to Mia and control her every step. Having spent years believing her baby girl had been stillborn, she now clung to the grown daughter that had miraculously been resurrected before her eyes.

"Well, it's a beautiful place," she finally said to him. "I'm sure you must love it here."

"It's nice" was his casual reply before he opened the door and climbed out to the ground.

After he helped her out of the vehicle and they began the short walk to the porch, Mia glanced expectantly around her. "I was expecting your dog to run out to meet us. Where is he?"

With his hand at her back, he ushered her up the three short steps to the porch.

"The backyard is fenced. That's where Leroy has to stay. Otherwise, he'd follow me down to the lodge and harass the guests."

"Oh," she said warily. "He bites?"

Marshall laughed. "No. But he'll knock you down trying to get your attention. I suppose I should send him to obedience school, but I'd miss him too much. And besides, none of us behave perfectly. Why should I expect Leroy to?

None of us behave perfectly. He couldn't have gotten that more right, Mia thought. But if he could see into her past behavior she doubted the doctor would have that same lenient compassion toward her.

Don't think about that now, Mia. Just enjoy the moment and bank this pleasant time in your memory. Once you leave Thunder Canyon and face your real life again, you're going to need it.

"We all have our bad habits," she murmured. "I'm sure Leroy is a nice boy."

Chuckling, he opened the door and ushered her over the threshold. "You've got it all wrong, Mia. I'm the nice boy around here and Leroy is the animal."

They passed through a small foyer furnished with a long pine bench and a hall tree adorned with several hats and jackets that she supposed would be needed once autumn came and the cold north winds began to blow across the mountains and plains.

"Oh, this is nice and cozy," she commented as they walked into a long living room with a wide picture window running along one wall.

Rustic pieces of furniture fashioned of varnished pine and soft butter-colored leather were grouped together so that the spectacular mountains could be viewed from any seat. Brightly colored braided rugs covered the oak flooring while the chinked log walls were covered with paintings and photos. Potted plants sat here and there around the room and from their lush appearance Mia figured he must have a green thumb along with his eye for the ladies.

"Well, I'm sure it doesn't compare to your home," he said, "but it suits me."

Pretending to study the view beyond the window, Mia looked away from him and hoped the mixed feelings swirling through her didn't show on her face.

It was true that Janelle's home was a mansion and large enough to hold several houses this size. But the last ratty apartment that she'd shared with Nina had been more of a home to her than any of those opulent rooms in Janelle's house. Funny that she could see that so clearly now when only a couple of years ago she'd believed Janelle was welcoming her into a castle in paradise. Dear God, she'd been so naive, so gullible, she thought.

"I think it's beautiful," she said, then turned to him and smiled in spite of the tears in her heart. "Where's the kitchen? I'll help you get things started."

"Whoa, slow down, pretty lady. We're going to relax and have a drink first. That is, after I change out of these work clothes. Why don't you have a seat and I'll be right back."

She was far too nervous to simply sit while

she waited for him to return. Clasping her hands behind her back, she said, "I think I'll just wander around the room and see how good you are about keeping things dusted."

"Lord, I'd better hurry," he said with a laugh and quickly darted through an open doorway.

Once he was gone from the room, Mia ambled slowly along the walls, curiously inspecting the many paintings that depicted the area and the cherished photos that were carefully framed and lovingly displayed. Eventually she discovered one of four smiling boys and an adult man, all of them dark-haired and all possessing similar features. The group had to be the Cates brothers and their father.

As she quietly studied their smiling features, she felt a pang of total emptiness in her heart. If Mia had been lucky enough to have siblings, her life would have no doubt taken a different track. Certainly she wouldn't have felt such a driving need to search for her birth mother. And with a sibling to lean on, Mia mightn't have been so profoundly influenced by Janelle. But ifs didn't count. And she'd not been as blessed as Marshall Cates.

Moments later, Marshall stepped through the door and spotted Mia at the far end of the room. Just seeing her there filled him with strange

emotions. He'd never invited one of his girlfriends here before and he wasn't exactly sure
why he'd felt compelled to blurt the sudden invitation to Mia. Something about her seemed
to make him lose all control and throw out all
the dos and don'ts he carefully followed with
other dates. The fear that he might be headed
for a big fall niggled at the back of his mind,
yet the sight of her slim, elegant body standing
in his living room was somehow worth the risk.

Obviously lost in his family photos, she
didn't hear him approach until he was standing
directly behind her. Resting his hands lightly
on her waist, he said in a teasing voice, "I see
you found the Cates brood. What do you think?
That we could pass for the wild bunch?"

She didn't answer immediately. Instead, she
turned and gave him a smile that was wobblier
than anything. The glaze of moisture in her
eyes completely dismayed him.

"You have a nice-looking family, Marshall,"
she said huskily. "You must love them very
much."

Before he could say anything, she eased out
of his grasp and stepped around him. As
Marshall turned to follow, he could she was
wiping a finger beneath her eyes. The image hit
him hard and he was stunned to discover his

throat was knotted with emotion. Why would seeing a photo of his family affect her like this? he wondered. And why was her tearful reaction tearing a hole right in his chest?

Clearing his throat, he caught her by the shoulder and gently pulled her to a standstill. "Mia? Are you okay?"

She lifted her face up to his and the smile he found plastered upon her delicate features was really just a cover-up and they both knew it.

"Of course I'm okay. I…I just get silly and sentimental at times. Don't pay any attention to me. Women get emotional. You ought to know that, doc."

Of course he understood women were emotional creatures, but as far as he could remember none of his dates in the past had ever shed a tear in front of him. The women he squired were more likely to have fits of giggles, a sign he must be dating good-time girls, he thought, then immediately wondered why that fact should fill him with self-disgust.

He glanced back at the photo of his family. Then, looking questioningly to her, he asked, "Do you have siblings?"

Shaking her head, she said, "No. I'm an only child."

She tried to smile again and this time her

soft lips quivered with the effort. Marshall was stunned at how much he wanted to pull her into his arms and soothe her. Not kiss or seduce her, but simply quiet her troubled heart. Something strange was definitely happening to him.

"I'm—sorry, Mia," he murmured. Then, quickly deciding he needed to put an end to the soppy moment between them, he urged her forward. "Come on," he said a bit gruffly. "Let's go have a drink and start dinner. I don't know about you, but I'm famished."

She seemed relieved that he'd suddenly changed the subject and by the time they reached the kitchen, she appeared to have pulled herself together. Marshall did his best to do the same as he went to the cabinet where the glasses were stored.

"Would you like a beer or a soda? I have a bit of everything stashed around here," he told her.

After a long pause, she answered. "I—uh, I really don't care much for alcohol."

Marshall looked over his shoulder to see she was resting her hip against the kitchen table, her long bare legs were crossed and she was studying him through lowered lashes. The provocative sight forced him to draw in a long, greedy breath of air.

"Oh. Since you visited the lounge, I didn't figure you had anything against drinking."

"I—" suddenly she straightened away from the table and glanced at a spot over his shoulder "—I have a weak cocktail on occasion. And I don't mind other people enjoying themselves. But it bothers me when it's abused."

Had she had trouble with overdrinking herself, Marshall wondered, then quickly squashed that question. She didn't seem the sort of woman to lose control over anything—even though that kiss they'd shared at the ice rink had been hot enough to sear his brain cells.

"Well, unfortunately we humans abuse a lot of things. Even food," he said.

"And people," she added in a small voice.

"Yeah, and people," he grimly agreed, then quickly shrugged a shoulder and grinned. "But we're not going to ruin our evening together by fretting over the ills of the world. Why don't I fix you a soda and I'll have a beer?"

Her smile was grateful. "Sounds good. Let me help."

Happy to change the solemn mood, Marshall gave her a glass to fill with ice then showed her where a selection of sodas was stored in the pantry. Once they had their drinks in hand, he ushered her out the back door and onto a wide deck made of redwood planks.

Almost instantly, she heard loud happy barks and turned around to see a stocky dog with a bobbed tail bounding onto the deck and straight at them.

"Leroy! Don't even think about doing your jumping act," Marshall warned the animal. "You sit and I'll introduce you to our guest."

The blue-speckled dog seemed to understand what his master was saying and Mia was instantly charmed as Leroy sat back on his haunches and whined happily up at her.

"Oh, you're gorgeous," she said to the dog, then glanced questioningly at Marshall. "Is it okay if I pet him?"

Marshall laughed. "That's what he's waiting for. But beware. He'll smother you if you let him."

Placing her soda on a small table, Mia leaned down and with both hands lovingly rubbed Leroy's head. "You're just a teddy bear," she cooed to the dog. "I'll bet you wouldn't hurt a fly."

"Maybe not a fly," Marshall said with amusement, "but he'd love to get his teeth around a rabbit or a squirrel."

Mia stroked the dog's head for a few more

moments then picked up her soda. Marshall waited until she'd settled herself on one of the cushioned lawn chairs grouped on the deck before he took a seat next to her.

Leroy crawled forward to Mia's feet, then rested his muzzle on his front paws. Smiling affectionately at the dog, she said to Marshall, "I'll bet he's a lot of company for you. Have you had him long?"

"Close to two years. I got him not long before I came to work here at the resort."

Mia glanced over at him and felt her heart lurch into a rapid beat. She'd been around handsome men before, but there was some indefinable thing about Marshall that sparked every womanly cell inside of her. It was more than the nicely carved features and the ton of sex appeal; there was a happiness about him that filled her with warm sunshine, a twinkle in his dark eyes that soothed the gaping wounds inside of her. Being with him filled her with a sense of worth, something she'd not felt since her father had died years ago.

Like Marshall, Will had been a happy man with a love for life. He'd always made a point of telling Mia that she was special, that she could do or be anything she wanted. He'd made her smile and laugh and look at the world as a place to be enjoyed. When she'd lost him, she'd also lost her self-confidence and security. But she wasn't going to think about that tonight.

"When was the resort built? There's so much to it that I figured the place had been here for several years."

Marshall shook his head. "Mr. Douglas didn't start building Thunder Canyon Resort until after gold was discovered in the Queen of Hearts mine, and that was about two years ago."

"Wow. He must have lit a fire under the contractors to have gotten the place up and running in such a short time."

"Yeah, well money talks and having plenty of it makes it easier to get things done quickly. Did you know there's a golf course in the makings, too? Construction is supposed to start on it next summer. Maybe when you come back to Thunder Canyon for another vacation we can play a game together. Have you ever played?"

Golf? Mia almost wanted to laugh. As far as she was concerned that was a rich man's sport. Even when Will, her father, had still been alive, the Hanovers hadn't been well off. The potato crops he'd harvested every year had been enough to keep them comfortable but not enough for luxury. Then after Will had died, she and Nina couldn't have afforded a set of used clubs from a pawnshop, much less the fees to belong to a country club. That was the sort of life Janelle enjoyed. It was the sort of life she wanted Mia to experience. But try as she might, Mia couldn't make herself comfortable with Janelle's money or lifestyle. How could she, when everywhere she looked she saw Nina Hanover's troubled face?

"No. I— Golf was never an interest at my home." At least that was the truth, she told herself.

The crooked smile on his face melted her. "Well, that will give me a good reason to get you out on the course and teach you."

If she ever returned to Thunder Canyon, Mia thought grimly. What would he think if he knew she was only here at the resort because of a missed turn on the wrong road? That she was running from herself and hiding from her mother? God, she couldn't bear to imagine how he would look at her if he knew the truth. That her actions had caused her mother to drink and then climb behind the wheel of a car.

Trying to shake the disturbing thoughts away, she sipped her soda and glanced around the small yard fenced with chain link. On the west side three poplars shaded them from the red orb of the sinking sun. To her left, in one corner of the grassy space, a blue spruce towered high above the roof of the house. Even from a distance, the pungent scent of its needles drifted to her on the warm breeze.

Near one end of the deck was a doghouse made with traditional clapboard and shingles. Nearby, a small wading pool meant for children was full of water—for Leroy's amusement, she supposed. A few feet farther, in the middle of the yard, a black gas grill was positioned near the end of a redwood picnic table.

The only thing missing in the family-friendly setting was a colorful gym set and a couple of laughing kids playing tag and wrestling with Leroy. The dreamy picture floated through her mind and filled her heart with wistful longing. Would there ever be a place like this for her? she wondered. Would there ever be a man who could love her and want a family with her in spite of her faults?

"Mia. Are you okay?"

His voice finally penetrated her thoughts and with a mental shake of her head, she glanced at him. Apparently she'd been so lost in her daydreams that she'd not heard his earlier remarks.

"Oh. Sorry. I was just thinking…how quiet

and pleasant it is here on the mountainside." Her expression turned wry. "But to be honest, this is not the bachelor pad I expected to find."

His eyes wandered over her face as he grunted with amusement. "What were you expecting? A round bed and mirrors on the ceiling?" His eyes crinkled at the corners. "Maybe I should remind you that you haven't seen my bedroom yet."

He was teasing and yet just the mention of his bedroom was enough to make Mia jump nervously to her feet and rub her sweaty palms down her hips. "Uh—maybe we should start dinner. I'm actually getting hungry."

Marshall set aside his empty beer glass, then slowly rose from the lawn chair. It was all Mia could do to stay put as he closed the short distance between them.

"Mia, Mia," he said softly as his hands slipped over the tops of her shoulders. "You really do think I eat women for breakfast, lunch and dinner, don't you?"

Embarrassed now, her gaze dropped to her feet. "Not exactly. But I'm sure you've had plenty of—female friends up here and—"

Before she could finish, his forefinger was beneath her chin, drawing her face up to his. "You're wrong, Mia. Very wrong. Yes, I've had plenty of female friends over the years. But not one of them has been here at my home. Until you, that is."

Something deep inside her began to quiver and she didn't know whether the reaction was from the touch of his hand upon her face or the surprising revelation of his words.

"Marshall, you don't have to tell me something like that. I mean— I'm not expecting special treatment from you."

Frowning now, his hand fisted and his knuckles brushed the curve of her cheekbone. Everything inside Mia wanted to close her eyes and lean into him. She wanted to taste the recklessness of his lips again, feel the strength of his arms holding her tight, crushing her body against his.

"You think I'm lying, don't you?"

Her head twisted back and forth until his fingers speared into her hair and flattened against the back of her skull. With his hands poising her face a few inches from his, everything in her went completely still. Except for her heart and that was beating as wildly as the wing of a startled bird.

"Marshall—it doesn't matter what I think."

"Doesn't it?"

She swallowed as emotions threatened to

clog her throat. "Soon I'll be gone and you and I will probably never see each other again."

Even saying the words brought a wretched loneliness to the deepest part of her heart and she suddenly realized she was in deep trouble with this man. It was painfully clear that he was becoming a part of her life, a part she didn't want to end.

"Mia," he said in a gravelly whisper, "when are you going to stop thinking about *leaving* and start thinking about *staying?*"

She couldn't stop the anguished groan in her throat. "Because I— Oh, Marshall, there's nothing to keep me here."

Mia had hardly gotten the words out when she saw a wicked grin flash across his face and then his lips were hovering over hers.

"What about this?"

His murmured question wasn't meant to be answered. At least not with words.

Mia closed her eyes and waited for his kiss.

Chapter Seven

Leaves rustled as a soft breeze blew down from the mountain, carrying with it the faint scent of spruce. Birds twittered overhead and across the deck Leroy lifted his head and watched in fascination at the couple with their arms entwined, their lips locked.

As for Mia, she was hardly aware of her surroundings. Marshall's kiss was spinning her off to a place she'd never been before, a place where everything was warm and soft and safe. The wide breadth of his chest shielded her, his strong arms girded her, cradled her as though she were something very precious to him.

Back and forth his lips rocked over hers, while inside tiny explosions of pleasure fizzed her brain, transmitting streaks of hot longing throughout her body.

Her hands were clinging tightly to his shoulders and she was wondering where she was ever going to come up with enough resistance to end the kiss, when he suddenly lifted his head. As she gulped for breath, his eyes tracked a smoldering trail across her face, down her neck, then still lower to the perky jut of her breasts.

"See, you do have something to keep you here," he murmured, his voice raspy with desire. "Me. This."

Mia was smart enough to know that Marshall wasn't an old-fashioned man. He considered a kiss as nothing more than a sexual pleasure between a man and a woman, a sweet prelude for something more intimate to come. It wasn't a pledge of love or even a promise of fidelity. For him it was a carnal act, plain and simple.

With every ounce of strength she could muster, Mia gathered enough of her senses to push away from his embrace and walk across the deck. Bending her head, she stared unseeingly at the grains in the wooden planks while asking herself what she was doing here at Marshall's home. Pretending that she could have that fairy-tale life she'd once fervently dreamed of? No. She'd learned the hard way that fairy tales weren't the heavenly fantasies she'd thought them to be. The reason she was here was far more basic. Marshall made her momentarily forget, made her feel as if she'd soon discover sunshine over the very next mountain.

She was blinking at the haze of moisture collecting in her eyes when Leroy's head appeared in her line of vision. The dog must have sensed her troubled mood. He looked up at her and whined, then promptly began to lick her ankles.

The warm, ticklish lap of the dog's tongue against her skin had Mia suddenly laughing and she squatted on her heels to stroke his head.

"You're a funny fellow," she crooned to Leroy.

Walking up behind her, Marshall put a hand beneath her elbow and eased her up to her full height. Slowly, she turned and met his somber gaze.

"I wish I could make you laugh like that," he said quietly. "It sounds nice. Really nice."

Feeling slightly embarrassed now, but not fully understanding why, she directed her gaze to the middle of his chest.

"I guess I'm not the most jovial person to be around, Marshall. I—" Pausing, she lifted her gaze back to his face. There was a smiling warmth in the brown depth of those eyes, a tenderness that she'd not expected to see and her heart winced with longing. "I really don't understand why you'd want to be around a person like me."

With a wry slant to his lips, his hand reached up and stroked gently over the shiny crown of her head then down the long length of her thick braid.

"A person like you? What does that mean? You're a beautiful, desirable woman. Any man would be crazy not to want your company."

Her nostrils gently flared as his fingers reached the end of her braid and lingered against her breast.

"Like I told you before, I'm not a party girl."

His palm flattened against her breast and Mia's pulse quickened as heat pooled beneath it and spread to the center of her chest.

"What makes you think that's the type of girl I want?" he murmured huskily. "Maybe I'm tired of party girls."

Why did she so desperately want to believe

him? Mia wondered. Why did the foolish, wishful part of her want to believe that he might actually come to care for her, when every sensible cell inside her brain understood that once her past was revealed he'd run faster than Leroy after a rabbit?

She sighed as a faint smile curved her lips. "That kiss you just gave me didn't feel like a man who was looking for a woman to share an evening of political theories. But I— I'll hang around Thunder Canyon for a while longer. Just don't expect me to fall in bed with you. That isn't going to happen."

To her surprise, a wicked grin flashed back at her. "What about jump into bed with me? Or leap? Yeah. Leap sounds better. That would get us there faster."

He was teasing and Mia was glad. It gave her a chance to step away from him and end the awkward intimacy that constantly seemed to sizzle between them.

"You're crazy," she teasingly tossed over her shoulder. "And right now I'm wondering if you actually know how to cook or if you're going to let me starve."

Chuckling, he draped his arm around the back of her waist and guided her down the steps and onto the grassy lawn.

"C'mon," he urged. "You can watch me start the grill and then I'm going to cook you the best rib-eye steak you've ever eaten."

Once Marshall got the charcoal burning, the two of them went inside the kitchen to prepare steaks, potatoes and corn on the cob for grilling. As Mia worked alongside him at the counter, she tried to push the heated memory of their kiss aside. She tried to convince herself that being in Marshall's arms hadn't really been that nice. But she couldn't lie to herself. Not when his very nearness begged her reach out and touch him.

They ate the simple meal on the picnic table while Leroy sat near Marshall's feet and begged for scraps. By the time they pushed back their empty plates, the sun was casting long shadows across the lawn.

"There's a little sunlight left," Marshall said as the two of them sipped the last of their iced tea. "Do you have enough energy for a walk? There's a beautiful little spot I'd like to show you. It's just a short distance up the mountain."

With a hand against her midsection, she groaned. "It had better be a short distance because I'm stuffed."

He extricated his long legs from the picnic bench and rose to his feet. "I promise the exercise will be good for your digestion," he said impishly, then held his hand down to her.

She curled her fingers around his and he helped her to her feet. "What about Leroy? Can he walk with us?" she asked as he led her over to a gate where they could exit the backyard.

Since the heeler was already bounding eagerly around their feet, Marshall didn't have the heart to order the dog back to the porch. Besides, Mia seemed to enjoy Leroy and whatever made her happy was what he wanted to give her.

Hell, if he ever admitted his sappy feelings to his brother and longtime buddies, the group of men would fall over with laughter, Marshall thought. Either that or warn him that he was in danger of losing his bachelorhood.

"If I didn't let him go, he'd probably dig out from beneath the fence," Marshall told her, then to Leroy he said, "okay, boy, you can go. But no running off and hiding in the woods or I'll leave you out for the bears to eat."

Leroy barked as though he was big enough to take on any black bear that happened to cross his path. The moment Marshall opened the gate, the dog shot through the opening like a rocket on four feet. Mia laughed as the animal raced far ahead of them.

"Boy, you've certainly got him trained."

"Yeah, he follows my directions about as well as my patients," he joked.

Marshall ushered her through the gate and onto a small trail leading out to the dirt road that ran past the house and on up the mountain.

"You mean we can walk on the road?" she asked with surprise. "We don't have to go into the woods?"

"For about a quarter of a mile we'll stick to the road," Marshall told her. "Then we'll turn into the woods. It won't be far then."

"And what will I see there?" she asked curiously.

He wagged a finger at her. "If I told you now, it wouldn't be a surprise when we got there. Don't you like surprises?"

When the surprises were nice, Mia thought. Like the ones her mother and father used to give her on her birthday: a kitten with a bow around its neck, a sweater with a fur collar and shiny pearl buttons, a small cedar chest to hold all her cherished trinkets. Yes, those had been precious surprises and gifts worth more than all the gold in the Queen of Hearts mine. She'd just been too naive to realize it at the time.

"Sometimes," she said.

They were walking close together and every

few moments the swinging gait of their arms caused them to brush together. Mia made herself widen the distance between them, but Marshall countered her move by reaching for her hand and dragging her even closer to his side.

As he threaded his fingers through hers, he said with a provocative little grin, "We're not on a military hike, Mia dear, we're on an after-dinner stroll."

The feel of her palm flattened against his and their fingers locked together was all it took to send Mia's blood singing through her veins. It was crazy, she thought. They were only holding hands, yet the connection she felt was almost as if they were kissing all over again. She wanted to pull away even while she wanted to draw closer to his side.

"It's a good thing," she said in a breathy voice. "Because I need to take this uphill grade slowly."

He was teasing her about being out of breath when they suddenly heard voices, then muffled whimpers. The sounds appeared to be coming farther up the mountain from them and Mia and Marshall paused long enough to exchange watchful glances.

"That sounds like someone in distress," Marshall said. "Is that what you heard?"

Concerned now, Mia nodded. "Is it unusual for anyone else to be on this road?"

"Not really. It's on resort property and some hikers like to go up the mountain the easy way rather than the narrow trail that winds through the woods. C'mon. Let's go see if we can find them."

He tugged on her hand and the two of them hurried up the steep road. Around a sharp curve, they spotted a boy no more than eight years old with taffy-brown hair and a smattering of freckles across his nose, sitting in the ditch. Tears were streaming down his face as a young woman with a light brown ponytail was trying to untie his hiking boot.

Mia shot Marshall a glance of concern, then rushed forward. The woman looked up in surprise as Mia practically stumbled to a stop in front of them.

"Oh, thank God," the young woman said with a desperate note of urgency. "Can you help us?"

"What's happened?" Mia asked quickly as she knelt down next to the woman.

"I'm not sure how it happened. Joey and I were walking through the woods and the next thing I knew he was on the ground screaming in pain."

"I was trying to jump a stream," the boy said in tearful explanation. "The next thing I knew I landed on a rock and it rolled beneath my boot. I fell and now my leg hurts something awful."

A grubby little hand rubbed down his shin and stopped somewhere near his ankle. Mia's heart ached for the little fellow. Apparently he'd taken quite a tumble. There were deep scratches on his knees and legs. Mud and dirt was smeared on his chin and alongside his nose.

The woman said fretfully, "Wouldn't you know it, this is the one time I didn't bring my cell phone with me. And Joey is too heavy for me to carry off the mountain."

Giving the boy a soothing smile, Mia reached into a pocket on her shorts and pulled out a clean tissue. Gently, she dabbed at the tears rolling down his cheeks, then went to work wiping away a trickle of blood from his knee. "You're a brave boy. Don't cry," Mia told him, turning toward Marshall who stood behind her. "This man is a doctor," she told Joey. "He'll take good care of you."

"A doctor!" Jumping to her feet, the woman stared at Marshall in disbelief. "Really?"

Marshall thrust his hand toward her. "I'm

Dr. Marshall Cates. I'm the staff doctor at Thunder Canyon Resort."

A look of relief crossed her plain features. "Oh. I'm Deanna. Deanna Griffin." She gestured down to the boy who was grimacing with pain. "And this is my son, Joey. We're not resort guests. We're staying in town at the Wander-On Inn. We just decided to drive out to the mountains and then Joey wanted to climb. I guess someone will probably charge us with trespassing."

"Don't worry about any of that," Marshall tried to assure her. "You're not going to get into trouble for being on resort property." Quickly, he broke off the conversation and kneeled down beside Mia and the boy. "Okay, Joey, can you show me where it hurts?"

The boy glanced to Mia for reassurance, then with a short nod pointed to his right ankle. "Somewhere down there. But it kinda just hurts all over. Is it broke?"

"I don't know, son. We'll have to take X-rays of your leg before we know that," Marshall told him.

Carefully, he cradled the bottom of the child's boot in both hands while anchoring his thumbs on the top. "Mia, can you loosen the laces while I keep his foot steady?" he asked.

Without hesitation she nodded, then gave the boy a conspiring wink. "Sure. We're gonna get through this together, aren't we, Joey?"

Gritting his teeth, Joey reluctantly nodded and Mia quickly went to work easing the bootlaces. Eventually she loosened them enough for Marshall to slip the shoe from the boy's foot. A thick white sock followed.

When Joey's foot was finally exposed, Marshall ran his fingers over the already bloated joint. "Mmm. The ankle is beginning to swell and turn blue. I don't feel anything broken." He glanced up at Joey's mother. "But there could be a fissure that can't be felt. We need to get him down to my office for X-rays."

Close to tears now, Deanna Griffin groaned with misgivings. Mia looked away from Joey and up to his mother. Although the woman was dressed in a decent-looking pair of Capris and a tank top, the look on her face spoke volumes to Mia. She'd seen that frantic what-am-I-going-to-do expression many times before on her own face. The fear in Deanna Griffin's eyes said she saw a mound of cost suddenly thrown at her, a cost she couldn't meet.

"Look, Dr. Cates, I think—maybe—I'd better have you take Joey to the county hospital. I'm not insured and, well, I hate to sound ungrateful but I don't think I can afford your services. At the hospital…"

The deep grimace on Marshall's face was enough to cause the woman to pause. "Ms. Griffin, this isn't about money," he said with rough impatience. "This is about your son's leg!"

Stunned by Marshall's attitude toward the woman, Mia touched him on the shoulder to get his attention. "Marshall, could I speak with you a moment? Alone?" she asked pointedly.

He hesitated for only a moment, then, leaving Joey, he followed Mia several feet away from the mother and son.

"What is it?" he asked before she could say anything.

Her lips pursed at his impatience. She was seeing a different side of this man and she wasn't at all sure she liked it.

Tossing back her tousled hair, she lifted her chin to a challenging slant. "For your information, Marshall, not all people are blessed with plenty of money like you. She's probably barely able to make ends meet and I doubt there's a man around to help her in any way. Now you bark at her as though she's an unfeeling mother!"

A look of impatience came over his face.

"Unfeeling! Mia, I was trying to tell the woman not to worry—that money isn't the issue here."

Stepping closer, she tapped a finger against the middle of his chest. "You still don't get it. Money *is* an issue with her. She doesn't have it. And medical care—the kind you provide—ain't cheap! Now do you get the picture?"

Frustration marked his features as he glanced over his shoulder at Joey then lowered his head to Mia's. "This woman is a stranger to you. How could you possibly know anything about her situation?"

Because she'd been there, Mia thought grimly. In that same dark, terrifying place with nowhere to turn and no one to help. Mia understood how humiliating and humble it felt to have to throw herself on the mercy of a total stranger. But she couldn't tell Marshall Cates about that part of her life. He wouldn't understand. No more than he could empathize with Ms. Griffin.

"It's…easy. I—I'm a woman and I can…just tell these things. And if she needs financial help, I'll be glad to pay for Joey's care."

Shaking his head with dismay, he raked a hand through his hair. "Mia, look. It's very generous of you to make the offer. But even if the kid has to spend time in the hospital, I have connections—I can make sure the bills are taken care of. Does that make you feel better?"

"Much better." Rising on tiptoe, she kissed his cheek, then hurriedly stepped past him and over to Joey's mother.

The woman turned a harried look on Mia. "Dr. Cates is right. Joey's leg is the first concern here. It's just that I have to be…uh, practical. And—"

"You don't have to explain, Ms. Griffin," Mia swiftly interrupted. "And there's nothing to worry about. Marshall meant to say that Joey will be treated and you're not to worry about the cost."

Her eyes blurred with grateful tears, Ms. Griffin reached out and gave Mia a tight hug. "I don't know what to say," she murmured. "Except thank you."

Mia was about to tell the woman that no thanks were necessary when Marshall approached the two women. "I think the best way to handle this is for me to jog back down the mountain and get the Jeep," he told Mia. "Can you wait here with Ms. Griffin and her son?"

"I'd be glad to."

His nod was grateful and as he turned to go, Mia thought she spotted a flicker of surprise in his eyes. As though he'd expected her to come up with some sort of excuse to quickly extricate herself from these people's problems. But Mia had learned that when a person cried out for help, someone needed to be there for them. This was one tiny way of making up for her mistakes.

"Good. I'll be back in a few minutes. In the mean-time, make sure Joey doesn't try to move or stand. If he does he could hurt himself even more."

"We'll make sure he stays put," Mia assured him.

Two hours later Mia and Marshall were sitting on the deck behind his house, drinking coffee and watching the stars come out.

Only minutes earlier on the lodge steps, they had waved goodbye to Joey and his mother. Thankfully, the boy's ankle had only been badly sprained. Marshall had ordered ice packs for the swelling and had made a point of giving Ms. Griffin samples of pain medicine rather than writing her a prescription.

"I'm sorry that we didn't make it to the special place I wanted to show you," he said to Mia. "We'll have to try again another day."

The two of them were sitting on a cushioned glider and every now and then Marshall would use the toe of his shoe to keep the seat rocking. The lazy movement, along with Marshall's nearness had lulled her to a dreamy state of mind and for the first time since Lance had left her, she felt herself drawing closer and closer to a man.

"I'm just glad we happened to run in to Joey and Deanna. The boy would have probably panicked if she'd left him there to go after their vehicle."

"Hmm. Well, I'm just glad the boy didn't have a broken bone. He was lucky." Marshall leaned forward and placed his coffee cup on the floor, then squared around to face Mia. "Now that things have quieted down, I want to compliment you on the way you handled Joey. A real nurse couldn't have done it any better. Where did that come from? Have you cared for children before?"

Mia very nearly laughed. The number of children she'd babysat to make extra money was too high to count. But heiresses didn't do those menial types of jobs, so she simply said, "I like children. I guess it's just a natural thing."

"I wouldn't say that," he argued. "When we walked up on them, his mother was getting nowhere at quieting him down."

She looked away from him and up at the blanket of stars twinkling across the endless Montana sky. There was so much she wished she could say to Marshall; so much she'd like to share with him, if only he would understand.

"That's nothing unusual. Most kids respond better to someone other than a relative. And I… Actually, at one time I was studying to become a nurse."

She glanced over to see he was staring at her in total surprise. What now?

"A nurse! Really?"

She swiftly sipped at her coffee to cover her nervousness. She didn't know why she'd blurted that bit of information about herself. "Yes. I'm very serious."

"You said you were studying. What happened? Why did you stop?"

What could she say, other than finding a rich mother had suddenly put a stop to all the goals and dreams she'd set for herself. Somehow she'd allowed Janelle to slowly take over her life, to push her into believing that being rich was all that was required for happiness.

Bitterness rose in her throat, but Mia did her best to swallow it down before she answered. "I guess in the long run you could say I stopped because I was weak. Too weak to fight my mother. You see, she, uh—she didn't want me doing something as blue-collar as being a nurse. To her a nurse does nothing more than hand out pills and empty bedpans."

Even though it was dark, there was enough light coming from the kitchen window for her to see that his brown eyes were searching her face as though she were a different woman than the one who'd first sat down beside him. As she sat there waiting for him to speak, she felt totally exposed and fearful that he was seeing the real Mia. Mia Hanover.

"I'm sorry she feels that way. I have a feeling you'd make a great nurse."

A nervous laugh escaped her lips and she quickly turned her head away from him. When she spoke her voice was wistful. "I wouldn't know about that, but I do think I would enjoy caring for people who…need me."

A few silent moments passed and then she felt him shifting on the seat and his arm settling around her shoulders.

"What about your father, Mia? Doesn't he have any say about this?"

This is the sort of thing that happened, she thought, when she let one little thing about herself slip. It always led to more questions. Questions that she didn't know how to answer without exposing her dirty secrets; questions that were too painful to contemplate.

Her next words were pushed through a tight throat. "My father died a long time ago."

"Oh, that's too bad, Mia. I can't imagine not having my father around. He's like an old tree trunk. I know I can lean on him if things ever get bad." His hand gently kneaded her shoulder. "Guess you have to do all your leaning on your mother."

Janelle wasn't the type, Mia thought. She wanted to lead her daughter rather than support her. Besides, she wasn't a mother to Mia. Not as Nina had been a mother. Nina was the one who'd bathed, diapered and fed Mia as a baby. She was the one who'd taken on multiple jobs; scraped and sacrificed to make sure Mia had a roof over her head and food to eat.

"I try not to do much leaning," she said. Then, with a smile she was hardly feeling, she quickly turned to him. "Let's not talk about such serious things, Marshall. You haven't offered me dessert yet. Do you have anything sweet hidden in your kitchen?"

"Sorry. The only thing I have is a package of cookies that has to be at least two months old."

Mia wrinkled her nose. "We could drive into

the Rusty Spur and share a carton of Golden Nugget," she suggested.

The last thing Marshall wanted to do was leave this quiet porch where Mia was practically sitting in his lap. From the moment they'd sat down together on the glider, the warmth of her body had been tempting him; the scent of her soft skin and silky hair cocooned him in a sensual fog. For the past half hour his mind and certain parts of his body had been zeroed in on making love to her. The idea of having her in his bed, her naked curves just waiting to be explored, was enough to leave his stomach clenched with need. It was all he'd been able to think about. Until she'd shocked him with that bit about nursing school.

Marshall had gotten the sense that she'd not intended to give him that information about herself, but now that she had, he only wanted more. He was beginning to see that there were layers to this woman he'd not even begun to see and he wanted to peel them away almost as much as he wanted to peel away her clothing.

But tonight was too soon to push her. She'd agreed to stay on at the resort for a while longer. For now Marshall had to be content with that.

Stifling a wistful sigh, he rose from the glider and offered a hand down to her. "Whatever my lady wants, I'm here to give."

Chapter Eight

The next evening, after Marshall had gotten off duty, he was walking through the lounge searching for any sight of Mia when his cell phone rang.

Flipping the instrument open, he was surprised to see it was his brother Mitchell calling. Quickly, he pushed the talk button as he continued to amble through the several couches and armchairs grouped in front of the massive fireplace.

"Hey, Mitch, what's going on?"

"What the hell do you mean, what's going on? We're all over here at the Hitching Post. Have you forgotten that it's our night to meet?"

Pausing at one of the empty cowhide-covered chairs, Marshall sank onto the padded arm. His brother's question had literally stunned him. How could he have forgotten boy's night out? For years now, Marshall, Mitchell, Grant and Russ and Dax had all gotten together once a month at the Hitching Post to drink beer, play pool and sit down to a game of poker. It was their time together, to relax and forget about any problems they might have. Just the idea that he'd been concentrating on Mia instead of his normal routine was enough to worry him.

"I suppose I had forgotten. Are you guys already gathered up?"

"Hell, yes. We were waiting on you to start the poker game, but the rest of the guys gave up and decided to play pool. What's the matter, did you have some sort of emergency this evening?"

"I'm still here at the lodge, I just stayed late to do a bit of paperwork." And to wait around and see if Mia made an appearance at the lounge, he thought wryly. Last night after they'd eaten ice cream, he'd dropped her off at her cabin and given her a chaste good-night kiss. He'd not wanted to press his luck and ask her for another date tonight, but he'd damned well wanted to. Dear Lord, if he'd missed boy's night out because of a date, the guys would never let him live it down. "Just hold my place, Mitch. I'll be there in a few minutes."

Friday night at the Hitching Post was always a rowdy affair with drinking, loud laughter and even louder music. The popular nightspot located on the southwestern edge of town was Thunder Canyon's version of an Old West saloon, complete with live country bands on Friday and Saturday nights and hardwood floors with plenty of space for boot stompin' and two-steppin'. A restaurant serving everything from steaks to burgers was situated on one side of the building, while on the opposite side was the original bar that had once graced Lily Divine's sporting house. And over the back bar, above the numerous bottles of spirits and rows of shot glasses, hung a painting of Thunder Canyon's most infamous lady.

Marshall, along with every guy who'd ever visited the Hitching Post, had often gazed at the nearly naked Lily and wondered if she'd really been as bawdy and decadent as the good folks of the town had depicted her to be back in the 1880s. There were always two sides to every story and he figured the truth of Lily's past would never be understood. The beautiful madam was a mystery. Just like Mia Smith, he thought, as he skirted the edge of the crowded dance floor and shouldered his way toward the bar. She was another beautiful mystery that he seriously wanted to unravel.

After wedging his way past the crowd packed around the busy bar, Marshall spotted his brother standing near one of the several pool tables located just off the dance floor.

He worked his way toward his brother while the band's rendition of a popular country tune rattled the rafters and forced people to communicate with hand signals rather than conversation. For one brief second, as he waited for a big burly cowboy to step aside, Marshall longed for the quiet sanctuary of his back porch, the glider and his arm around Mia.

Hell, what was coming over him, Marshall wondered as he finally reached the pool table where his brother and friends were racking balls for a new game. He'd always loved the nightlife, the louder and wilder, the better. The Hitching Post had given him some damn good memories and getting together with his brother and buddies was a tradition since their high school days. This was his idea of the good life and he didn't want to change a damn thing about it.

"Hey, buddy, you finally made it," Grant Clifton called to him from the opposite end of the table. "Want to play this game?"

Russ Chilton, the rancher of the group, took the pool stick he'd been leaning on and offered it to Marshall. "Go ahead. I've already lost one game to the stud down there." He motioned his head toward Grant. "Why don't you see if you can wipe that smug smile off his face?"

"Aw, Russ, the smile on Grant's face doesn't have anything to do with beating you at pool." Dax Traub, spoke up over another blast of loud music. "The man is in love. Real, true love."

Marshall looked across the table at Dax, who owned a motorcycle shop in the old part of town. The remarks he'd made about Grant's love life had held more than a hint of cynicism, but that was to be expected from Dax. He was six foot of brooding sarcasm since his marriage to Allaire had hit the skids.

"How do you know so much about Grant's love life?" Marshall asked at the same time as he signaled to a nearby waitress.

Dax jerked his thumb toward Grant. "The big manager of Thunder Canyon Resort has been telling us all about his upcoming wedding to his cowgirl. I've advised him to take her spurs off first, though. Otherwise she might trip on her way down the aisle."

By now the waitress had reached Marshall. He quickly ordered a beer, then turned and walked to where Grant was resting a hip against the edge of the pool table.

"Sounds like Dax is giving you a hard time about becoming a husband," Marshall said with faint amusement.

Grinning, Grant tossed his pool stick to Dax. The other man quickly positioned himself over the table and busted the triangle of balls.

With the game going again, Grant moved a few steps away from the table and Marshall followed.

"I wouldn't expect anything else from Dax. He's jaded."

Marshall blew out a lungful of air. Even though he'd known that Grant was engaged, the idea that his old buddy would soon be married shook him in a way he'd never expected. Grant's bachelor days were coming to an end.

Marshall glanced shrewdly at his longtime friend. "Maybe Dax is concerned that you'll end up getting hurt—like him. But I'll have to say you don't look like a worried man."

Grant chuckled. "Worried. Why should I be? I'm marrying the woman I want to spend the rest of my life with. I couldn't be happier."

Marshall slapped a hand on Grant's shoulder. "If you're happy, then I'm happy for you."

"Thanks. Maybe you can deliver our children when they come," Grant added jokingly.

With a wry shake of his head, Marshall said, "I'm a sports doctor, Grant. Remember? I don't do babies."

Grant's calculating laugh was loud enough to be heard above the music. "Maybe not in the delivery room. But you might just make a few—if you meet the right woman."

Marshall didn't think he'd ever seen his longtime friend so buoyant and happy. Nor had he ever heard him talk so openly about love and kids, subjects that normally would have made both men squirm. Now Marshall could merely look at him and wonder.

Glancing toward the other members of their group, Marshall said, "You know me, Grant, I'm never really looking for the *right* woman. But I— I'm half afraid that I may have found her anyway."

The waitress arrived with his beer and he tossed a few bills onto the serving tray before she hurried off to deliver more drinks.

As he gratefully sipped the dark draft beer,

Grant edged closer. "What do you mean? I didn't realize you'd been seeing one certain woman."

Feeling more than a little foolish, Marshall shrugged. "I hadn't been. But then I ran into Mia and we—uh—we've gone out a few times." He glanced at Grant and appreciated the fact that his friend wasn't grinning like a possum. "This is probably going to sound crazy, Grant, but I think I'm falling for this girl."

Grant's dark brows lifted with surprise. "Mia? Do I know this woman?"

"You should. Her name is Mia Smith. She's one of the high-toned guests at the resort. I remember you said she rented a safety deposit box for her jewelry."

Grant's lips formed a silent *O*. "Yeah, I remember now. The mystery heiress that all the staff was chattering about when she first arrived. You've been seeing her?"

Marshall nodded. "Believe me, Grant, I never thought she'd give me the time of day. Now that she has I—well, all I want is to be with her. And if I'm not with her I'm thinking about her. Does that sound like love to you?"

Frowning, Grant said, "Marshall, from what I've heard about Mia Smith, she keeps to herself. No one around the resort knows where she came from or anything else about her. Do you?"

What little Marshall knew about Mia was hardly enough to fit in his eye, yet he'd learned enough to tell him she was a good, decent person and that being with her made him happy. Wasn't that really all that mattered, he asked himself. To Grant he admitted, "I've learned a little about her, but not as much as I'd like to."

Slapping a comforting hand on Marshall's shoulder, Grant said, "Well, I wouldn't worry about it, ole buddy. You're probably just infatuated with her because she's a mystery. Once you give yourself time to really get to know the woman, your feelings might change completely."

After a long gulp of beer, Marshall glanced out at the crowded dance floor. For the life of him he couldn't imagine Mia laughing and kicking up her heels like the women here at the Hitching Post were doing tonight. She'd said she wasn't a party girl, but Marshall instinctively felt there was more to her reserved mindset than what she was telling him.

"You may be right, Grant. The only thing I'm sure about now is that I'm going to keep seeing her—until she leaves the resort."

Several loud shouts suddenly sounded from the pool table and both men returned to the group of friends just in time to see Dax send the last ball on the table rolling into a corner pocket.

Looking for anything to get his mind off Mia, Marshall said, "Give me that cue, Russ. Somebody needs to knock Dax off his throne."

More than an hour later and after several games at the pool table, the five guys found seats and ordered pitchers of beer.

As for Marshall, he tried to keep up with the bits and pieces of conversation flowing back and forth across the table, but all the while he was wondering what sort of believable excuse he could come up with to leave the party early.

He could always pull out his cell phone and pretend he had an emergency message from the resort. But with Grant being the manager, he'd eventually find out the truth and then his departure would need even more explanation. Damn it, why couldn't he just sit back and enjoy himself like he usually did at these gatherings?

The next thing Marshall knew, Dax was waving a hand in front of his face. "Hey, buddy, are you with us?"

Realizing he'd been caught daydreaming,

Marshall placed his beer mug on the table and glanced around the table. "I'm here," he answered a bit sharply. "I was just thinking about a patient," he lied. "Did you ask me something?"

"Yeah, we want to know about your date with Lizbeth Stanton. What was that all about?"

Grimacing, Marshall asked, "How did you know about that?"

Russ laughed. "Since when did anything stay a secret around Thunder Canyon? You ought to know Dax hears a stream of gossip in his motorcycle shop."

Marshall shrugged. "Well, there wasn't anything to it. She asked me out to dinner and I accepted. No big deal. She's really more of a friend than anything."

"Sexy as hell, though, don't you think?" Dax tossed a wink at him. "And she's just your style—a big flirt."

Marshall was about to tell him to go jump off a cliff when he spotted Mitchell staring at him like a hound dog with perked ears.

"You say Lizbeth asked you out?" his brother asked. "Not the other way around?"

"That's right," Marshall answered. "But like I said, the two of us are just friends. In fact, while we were having dinner she encouraged me to go after Mia Smith."

"I see."

Marshall thoughtfully watched his brother tip the pitcher of beer over his near-empty glass. If he didn't know better, his brother seemed unduly interested in Lizbeth Stanton, but that idea was ludicrous, he thought. Mitchell was the serious one. Flirty, flighty Lizbeth would be the last woman to fit his needs.

"Oh, so you've already moved on to this Mia now?" Dax asked. "Maybe we should be asking about her instead of Lizbeth."

Rising to his feet, Marshall pulled several bills from his trouser pocket and tossed them onto the table to pay for his portion of the beer.

"Sorry guys. I've had a long day and there's a patient I want to check on before it gets too late."

"A patient! Are you kidding?" Grant exclaimed. "Since when did you ever worry about a patient after working hours?"

Since he'd met Mia, Marshall silently answered. Aloud, he said, "There's a first time for everything, guys."

He walked away, leaving every man at the table staring after him.

The next morning Mia had just stepped out of the shower and was toweling dry when she heard a knock on the door of her cabin.

Puzzled that anyone would be trying to contact her, she quickly pulled on a blue satin robe and knotted the sash at her waist as she hurried to the living area.

Even though the resort was basically safe and away from the dangers that lurked in city living, she still opted to use the peephole before simply pulling the door open to a stranger. But to her surprise the visitor wasn't a stranger. It was Marshall, dressed in a green short-sleeved shirt and faded blue jeans. The tan cowboy boots on his feet reminded her that even though the man was a doctor, he still had a bit of Montana in him. And it was that rough edge that made him just too darn sexy for a woman's peace of mind.

Her pulse fluttering wildly, she thrust strands of wet hair off her face and pulled open the door to find him smiling back at her.

"Good morning, beautiful," he said softly.

The sweet, sensual greeting knocked her senses for a loop. Embarrassed that he'd caught her in such a disheveled state, she clutched the folds of her robe chastely together at the base of her throat.

"Hello yourself," she replied while her mind spun with questions. What was he doing here at her cabin so early in the morning? And why did the sight of him make her heart sing? She was clearly losing control with him—and herself.

"Uh—I know it's early. I tried to call, but there was no answer." His dark gaze left her face to travel downward to where her puckered nipples were outlined by the satin, then farther down to where the edges of the fabric parted against one naked thigh. "I guess you were in the shower—or something."

Just before Mia had stepped into the shower she'd heard her cell phone ringing, but even though she'd given her number to Marshall the other night after they'd dealt with Joey's sprained ankle, she'd figured the only person who would be calling so early was Janelle. And Mia was still far from ready to talk to the woman.

"Yes, I was in the shower," she repeated as though she didn't have an ounce of brain cells. Then, realizing she couldn't keep him standing on the small porch, she pushed the door a bit wider. "Would you like to come in?"

The grooves in his cheeks deepened as he

stepped across the threshold and past her. "I thought you'd never ask," he said as he glanced thoughtfully around the small but luxuriously fitted cabin.

Her hands shaking, she shut the door behind them and then adjusted the front of her robe to a more modest position.

"This is quite a surprise," she said. "I wouldn't have expected you to be up so early on a Saturday morning. Would you like coffee?"

She moved around him and into the kitchen. Thankfully she'd turned on the coffeemaker before she'd stepped into the shower and now the brew was ready to drink.

"I'd love a coffee," he said as he followed her behind an L-shaped bar and into the small kitchen area. "And this might surprise you, but I'm not one to lay in bed on my days off. There's too much to enjoy and life's too short to sleep it away."

Grateful that the task of finding cups and pouring the coffee gave her a moment to collect herself, she said in a teasing voice, "Oh. Well, I figured with your nightlife you'd need the rest."

He chuckled. "Nightlife? Now who's been talking about me? I don't have that much of a nightlife. Even though I was out last night—at the Hitching Post with my brother and friends."

Turning, she handed him one of the mugs. Their fingers met and at the same time their gazes clashed. For a brief moment Mia's breath stopped, as arcs of sizzling awareness seemed to zip back and forth between them.

"Friends?"

She realized the question was personal, that it was the same as saying *I'm interested in you,* but she couldn't stop herself. If he'd been out with another woman last night, then his showing up here this morning wouldn't be anything for her heart to sing about. Maybe it wasn't anything to sing about anyway. But she couldn't seem to get her heart to go quiet. Instead it was thumping and jumping joyously around in her chest.

"My old high school buddies." A corner of his mouth slanted upward. "Guys—just in case you're wondering."

Feeling a blush coming on, she lifted the cup to her lips and sipped while she waited for the heat in her cheeks to subside.

"I guess it's time to confess that I have heard gossip about you."

One of his dark brows arched with amused speculation. "Really? Where?"

She lowered the cup and tried to keep her voice casual. "The Clip 'N' Curl."

Marshall laughed. "The beauty salon in town? Mia, you're *supposed* to hear gossip at a beauty salon. Something would be wrong if you didn't."

She did her best to chuckle along with him. Yet these past few days she'd not been able to completely dismiss what Marti had revealed about her sister and Marshall.

"This particular person I met there seemed to know you quite well. Or, at least, her sister did."

His amusement turned to outright interest. "You don't say. Well, who was this person?"

"Marti Newmar. She works at the coffee bar in the lounge."

Sudden dawning crossed his face and then he glanced down at the cup in his hand, but not before Mia glimpsed something like regret in his eyes.

"Hmm. Marti. Yes, I'm acquainted with her. And yes, I dated her older sister, Felicia. It was nothing serious, though, and she's gone on to other things. In fact, I don't even think she lives here anymore."

He sounded so casual, almost too casual. And a prick of warning sent a cool shiver down her spine. If he was that flippant about his past girlfriends, then who was to say he'd be any different with her?

But you don't want him to be serious about you, Mia. You're a fake, a phony. Even if he did grow to love you, the truth would end everything. No, a mild flirtation is as far as this thing with Marshall could ever go.

Sighing, she leaned against the bar and stared across the expanse of living room. "Marti seems to think that her sister was in love with you."

She could hear his boots shifting slightly, but she didn't turn to look at him. If she saw another dismissive look on his face she didn't think she could bear it.

"I couldn't help that, Mia. Felicia was—she wasn't my type. I'm at fault for dating her in the first place."

"Why wasn't she your type?" Mia asked stiffly. "Because she was poor?"

"Poor? You think that's why I ended things with her?"

There was such indignation in his voice that she glanced over her shoulder at him. He was glowering at her and she knew she'd hit a nerve, but at this moment she didn't care. Maybe it was time Dr. Playboy was questioned about his dating ethics.

"I don't know," she said. "From the way

Marti describes her home and family, it doesn't match up to yours."

"Well, the Newmars' financial situation had nothing to do with anything," he countered. "Felicia was—naive. That was the whole problem."

Mia's lips twisted. She'd been naive before, too. She'd been foolish to believe that Lance had loved her enough to stick with her through the good and the bad. But even worse, it had been silly, perhaps even childlike, to believe that Janelle and her stacks of money could buy happiness.

"Why?" she asked, her voice brittle. "For believing a guy like you could care about a girl like her?"

He groaned. "Why are you trying to make me look like a cad?"

With a shake of her head, she said, "I'm not trying to do anything. Maybe you've already done it to yourself."

There was a pregnant pause and then she heard a rough sigh escape him.

"Look, Mia, you're probably right in thinking that I hurt Felicia. I'm sure I did. But I didn't do it intentionally. I never led her on or tried to make her believe she was *the* special woman in my life. She was simply a pretty girl, a fun date. But she obviously wanted more than I was prepared to give. When I finally saw where her feelings were headed, I quickly ended things. If that makes me an unfeeling bastard, then I guess I'm guilty."

Feeling a bit raw without even knowing why, she said, "Forget it, Marshall. I shouldn't have brought the matter up anyway. You and I are just friends. And your past dating habits are no concern of mine. No more than mine are yours."

Chapter Nine

Before Marshall could say any more on the subject of Felicia Newmar or any other women he'd dated, Mia turned toward him and gestured to one of the tall bar stools pushed up against the varnished pine counter.

"Have a seat," she invited.

He pulled out one of the bar stools and slung a long leg over the padded seat. Mia placed her coffee mug on the bar, then carefully climbed onto the stool next to him. As he sipped at his coffee, she pulled a wide-tooth comb from the pocket of her robe and began to smooth the wet tangles away from her face.

As Marshall watched her deal with the mass of black hair tousled around her head, he couldn't help but wonder why she'd confronted him about an old girlfriend and why he'd felt so compelled to defend himself. Before Mia, he'd not really cared what anyone thought of his dating habits. If a heart got broken here and there, he'd justified his part in the malady by telling himself the woman had learned a lesson about men, albeit the hard way. But now, to even think of breaking Mia's heart troubled him deeply. Dear God, what was she doing? Taking a freewheeling bachelor and turning him into a conscientious but boring gentleman?

"I thought you might like to know that I stopped by the Wander-On Inn last night and checked on Joey," he commented. "His ankle is coming along nicely."

She looked at him with surprise. "You mean you interrupted your night on the town to check on a patient?"

A wry smile twisted his lips. "You see, I'm not all bad, as you seem to think."

"I never thought you were *all* bad."

Their gazes clashed and her eyes darted nervously away from him. He watched her put down the comb and pick up her coffee.

"I would offer to make you breakfast," she said after a moment, "but I don't have any food in the house. I'm afraid I've been doing too much eating out, letting others do the cooking."

"Don't worry about it. I actually stopped by to invite you out, anyway. I thought we could grab some breakfast at the Grubstake and then do a bit of climbing."

Her gaze swung back to him. "Climbing? As in mountain climbing?"

He grinned at her wariness. "Sure. You're up to it, aren't you?"

Even though he had mentioned the two of them going climbing together before, Mia had never believed he'd actually get around to asking her. Taking an inexperienced person on such a strenuous trek would be like taking a toddler on a shopping excursion.

"I don't know." She licked her lips as she weighed his invitation. Mia Smith, the heiress who wanted to stay hidden from the world, knew it would be wise to politely decline and send him on his way. But she was getting so weary of being that woman, so tired of pretending. And more importantly, it didn't matter to her what this man's motives to spend time with her were; being with Marshall simply made her feel good. And right now she needed that very much.

She said, "You've surprised me."

"Good. A man shouldn't be predictable." His eyes sparkled with all sorts of innuendos. "At least, not to a beautiful woman."

Her nostrils flared as her pulse fluttered. It would be so much easier if she could forget the taste of his lips, forget the feel of his strong arms wrapped around her, but she couldn't and now as she looked at him her senses buzzed with erotic memories. This was probably how Marti's sister had felt, she thought, charmed, helpless, ready to give the man anything he wanted.

"I'll go climbing with you. Just as long as you don't try to take me up something like Pike's Peak."

Marshall chuckled. "The highest mountain in Montana is Granite Peak and it's many miles east of here. We'll go up a baby mountain here on the resort. Promise." He used his forefinger to make a cross against his chest, then leaning toward her, he wound a strand of wet hair around the same finger. "You ought to know I wouldn't hurt a hair on your head."

Even though Mia desperately needed to draw in a deep breath, the air lodged in her throat. "I'm—um. It's not my hair that I'm concerned about. It's my bones."

A deep chuckle rumbled up from his chest and his finger left her hair to slide down the stretch of thigh exposed by the part in her robe. "I'm a sports doctor, remember? I can fix broken bones."

Yeah, but what about broken hearts? Don't think about it, Mia. Just go. Have fun. Forget.

Carefully, she caught his wayward hand and placed it safely on his knee. "All right, doc," she conceded. "You've talked me into it. What time did you want to go?"

His smile was a picture of pure triumph. "Great! I'm ready right now."

Mia glanced pointedly down at her robe. "Well, I'm not. You're going to have to give me time to get dressed. What should I wear?"

"You might want to settle on loose-fitting shorts. It's going to be a warm, sunny day."

Mia quickly slipped off the bar stool. "Give me five minutes," she told him.

Just as she was walking across the living room, her cell phone began to ring. Mia glanced at the small table where the device was lying and felt her spirits sink. Janelle had been ringing and ringing, no doubt determined to make Mia pick up and talk to her. So far, she'd not found the courage or determination to confront her mother.

"Go ahead," Marshall spoke up from his seat at the bar. "I'm not in that big of a hurry. Answer your phone."

Knowing it would look odd if she didn't acknowledge the ringing, Mia picked up the phone and flipped it open. The caller ID flashed the name Janelle Josephson and her heart sunk all the way to her toes.

Snapping the phone shut, she said, "I— It's nothing important. I'll return the call later."

The ringing stopped and Marshall watched her place the phone back on the table. Her features, which only a moment ago had been smiling, had rapidly gone pensive, then guarded. Who could the caller be, he wondered. A family member? A lover? All along he'd sensed that something was going on with Mia Smith, something that she wanted to keep hidden.

He figured the answer could be found if he sifted through the call history information on her telephone. A name. A number. Someone from her past was obviously still reaching out to her. He desperately wanted to know, but he couldn't push her. He had to be patient and wait to see if she would ever feel close enough to confide in him.

"Are you sure? We have all day for climbing," he tried to assure her.

Suddenly she snatched the instrument up from the table again and this time slipped it into the pocket on her robe. "It's nothing important, Marshall," she said in a firm voice, then whirled and started out of the room. "Just let me change and we'll be on our way."

Marshall was still thinking about her odd behavior when she emerged from the bedroom a few minutes later wearing a pair of black khaki shorts and a white tank top. A white scarf secured her wet hair into a ponytail at the nape of her neck.

Even with a bare minimum of makeup her face was lovely, but at the moment it wasn't her features that had snared his attention. With a will all their own, his eyes slid an appreciative gaze down her long, shapely legs and ended as her trim ankles disappeared into a pair of heavy brown hiking boots. The sight of all that honey-tanned skin was enough to distract him from the earlier phone call and he put it entirely out of his mind as he slid from the bar stool and walked over to her.

"Ready to go?" he asked.

Nodding, she patted the back pockets of her jeans. "I think I've taken everything I needed from my hand-bag." She glanced eagerly up at him. "Is Leroy going to come with us?"

Laughing, he placed a hand at the small of her back and guided her toward the door. "Not this time. I want to devote all my attention to you, dear Mia."

After a quick breakfast of hotcakes, they left the Grubstake and climbed into Marshall's Jeep for a short drive to the north edge of the resort. Before they reached the base of the mountain, a meadow carpeted with pink and yellow wild-flowers came into view and Mia gasped with delight.

"Oh, how beautiful! Can't we stop here for a few minutes, Marshall?"

An indulgent smile curved his lips. "We'll make a visit here on the way back," he promised. "I'm afraid if I let you wander out in all those flowers now, I'll never get you up the mountain."

She sighed as she gave the splendorous sight one last glance before she turned her gaze on his profile. "You're probably right, doc. Most women tend to prefer picking flowers to climbing rocks. But I'm game and I'll try to keep up."

Reaching across the small console, he picked up her hand and gently squeezed. "You're a good sport, Mia. I like that about you. Believe it or not, you're the only woman who's been brave enough to go climbing with me."

His admission warmed her heart, even though she told herself it shouldn't mean anything.

"Maybe you mean the only woman *crazy* enough to go climbing with you," she said with a wry smile.

His fingers tightened around hers. "You're not crazy, Mia. You're an adventuress. I knew that when I first saw you sitting on that boulder on the side of the mountain. A weaker woman wouldn't have even attempted that much of a climb. You not only made it, but you made it alone. I was impressed."

Mia's lashes fluttered downward to partially hide her mixed emotions. He'd called her an adventuress and that much was true. Even before she'd graduated high school, she'd set off on a quest to find her real mother. In spite of having limited funds, even more limited means of searching and her adopted mother's disapproval, she'd been determined, almost relentless in reaching her goal. She'd been brave enough to make calls to total strangers and badger those persons holding the key to private records. Yet once she'd actually found Janelle, her bravery and independent nature had melted. She'd allowed the woman and her money to very nearly swallow her up. It had taken Mia months and months to realize that her weakness had not only caused her to lose Nina and Lance, it had also caused her to lose herself.

Lifting her head, she did her best to push the dark thoughts from her mind. "You didn't give me any impression that you felt that way," she replied.

"I didn't know you well enough. And you weren't exactly inviting me to strike up a personal conversation."

No, she thought miserably, when she'd first arrived at Thunder Canyon Resort, she'd gone out of her way to keep every encounter with staff and guests to a totally impersonal level. It was easier to maintain her guise as Mia Smith that way. But now Marshall was digging at the doors she was hiding herself behind and every moment she was with him she had to fight to keep from flinging them open and letting Mia Hanover pour out. The only thing stopping her was knowing the deluge of truth would end their relationship.

"So," she said carefully, "do you think you know me now?"

To her surprise, he lifted her fingers to his lips. "Not as much as I'd like to, but enough to make me want you beside me."

No one had to tell her that Marshall Cates was a dangerous flirt, a smooth charmer. Yet none of that seemed to matter whenever he touched her or flashed her one of his sultry grins. Mia realized she was losing herself to him and there didn't seem to be any will inside her to stop the fall.

Moments later, he steered the Jeep onto a dim, washed-out road that led up the base of the mountain. When the going finally became too rough for the vehicle to handle, he steered it off the path and parked beneath a huge pine.

She helped Marshall unload the climbing equipment from the back of the Jeep, then stood to one side and watched as he strapped on a heavy backpack.

"What about me?" she asked. "Do I need to carry something?"

"You can be in charge of our water. Since I only brought two bottles, they shouldn't be too heavy."

"Two bottles? The day feels like it's going to be hot. Won't we be needing more water than that?"

He glanced at her as he adjusted the pack to a more comfortable position on his shoulders. "You're right, but trying to carry too much of it will only weigh us down. I've brought a filtration device along, too. And once we climb higher, there are several falls and pools where we can get water."

She looked at him with fascination. "There are pools of water up on the mountain?"

"Several," he answered as he took her by the arm and urged her away from the Jeep. "And one of them will make your flowered meadow look humdrum."

"I'll believe that when I see it," she said with a laugh.

The day was bright and sunny, the breeze warm and gentle. The first two hundred feet of their climb were strenuous but fairly easy to maneuver with plenty of hand- and footholds. Thankfully Mia was accustomed to jogging in the high altitude of Denver, so her breathing was no more labored than Marshall's as they levered and worked their way upward. During the slow climb he'd made sure to stop at frequent intervals to give her some lessons on the basic techniques. Apparently his instructions had been a big help to her, because each time he'd glanced over his shoulder to make sure she was keeping up and each time she'd surprised him by being right on his heels.

Eventually he paused long enough for her to join him on a small rock ledge. "I think it's time I made our trail a little more difficult," he said. "This is no challenge for you."

Groaning, she shrugged off the small pack she was carrying and dug inside for one of the water bottles. "C'mon, Marshall, give me a break. I'm already covered with sweat."

While she took a long drink from the bottle, a cunning grin flashed across his tanned face. "You haven't done any real climbing yet. We're going to get out the anchors and ropes and make our way up that bluff."

Mia's gaze followed the direction of his index finger. When she spotted the bluff he was talking about, her jaw dropped. The red layers of rock appeared to be shaved off evenly without even the smallest of ledges to give a climber a toehold.

"You're crazy!" she squeaked. "I can't make it up there! Just look at my boots, they don't have spikes!"

"Neither do mine. In fact, I wore these old cowboy boots today and they're slick on the bottom and hell to climb in."

Mia rolled her eyes. "Then why did you wear them?"

"For a challenge. And to put me on an even keel with you."

She let out another groan. "And here I was

patting myself on the back for keeping up with you. I didn't have a clue that you'd handicapped yourself."

Chuckling, he reached out and cupped the side of her face with his palm. "You're doing great, honey. I'm proud of you."

Shaken by the sweet sensation of his touch, she handed the water to him, then turned away to gaze out at the quaint town of Thunder Canyon spread beneath the endless stretch of blue Montana sky. Months ago, after Lance had walked away and her mother had died, she'd believed that no spot on earth would feel like home again. But this place was beginning to tug at her heart.

Or was it the man standing beside her?

"Maybe you'd better wait until we tackle the bluff before you say that," she told him.

He moved closer and Mia's eyelids drifted down as the back of his hand moved against her bare arm.

"You're going to make it," he murmured. "We'll make it together."

Together. It was difficult for Mia to remember back to a time when she'd thought of herself as a part of a team. She had a few female friends back in Denver, but they were Janelle's sort, spoiled and out of touch with the real world. They'd readily accepted her into their circle and all of them were basically nice to her, but she'd never felt a connection with any of them and she'd quickly come to the conclusion that she didn't want an idle life without goals or dreams. As for the young men who'd tried to court her, she'd felt frozen by their flippant attitude toward life and money and family.

"Mia? You've grown awfully quiet. Are you all right?"

She glanced over her shoulder and up at him. The look of concern on his face warmed her and made her wonder what it would be like if he really did care about her, even love her.

"I was just thinking," she said, then before she could stop herself, she twined her arm through his. "Tell me about your friends, Marshall. The guys you went out with last night. Are they—special to you?"

A look of real fondness swept over his features. "Very special. We all grew up together—went to high school together and even now we make sure we all get together at least once a month. 'Course, I call Mitch my brother and my friend. He's four years younger than me and a hell of a lot smarter. He owns and runs Cates International in Thunder Canyon."

"That's some sort of business?"

"Farming equipment." His expression turned wry. "Not everyone around here has a gold mine where they can harvest nuggets."

"Is your brother married?"

Marshall's laugh was robust to say the least. "No. He's as serious as a judge. I'm not sure any woman could deal with him."

"What about your friends? Do they have families?"

He thought for a moment. "Not exactly. Dax used to be married to Allaire, but their marriage didn't last. Now he runs a motorcycle shop down in the old part of town. Then there's Grant, I think I told you about him. He manages the resort. He's a workaholic, but he's finally managed to get himself engaged to the woman who runs his ranch, Clifton's Pride. Russ has a ranch outside of town. He's from the old school—hates everything the gold rush has brought to Thunder Canyon. He used to be married a long time ago and has a kid—a son— but he never sees him."

Mia frowned. "How sad."

"Yeah. I think his ex didn't want the connection—I'm not sure. Russ doesn't talk about that part of his life. Anyway, he's definitely single and I don't see him changing."

"So that's all of them? Your friends, I mean."

"No. There's also Dax's brother, DJ, but he took off to Atlanta and has been living down there for a while. He owns a bunch of barbecue places and we've been trying to talk him into coming back to Thunder Canyon. What with the gold boom, a barbecue joint around here ought to do handsprings."

Mia smiled wistfully. "You're lucky to have friends and especially lucky that you've stayed together for so long."

"I'm sure you must have good friends, too." He grinned impishly. "I'll bet you were the prom queen or the cheerleading captain—someone that all the girls envied."

Mia had to stop herself from snorting out a laugh. She'd been tall, skinny and gawky. Her clothes and shoes had mostly come from thrift stores and her hair had been worn with thick bangs and chopped off straight at the bottom because that was the only way her mother could cut it. A visit to the beauty salon had been out of the question. Necessities came first and there was rarely a dollar left over for luxuries. No, none of the girls she'd gone to school with had envied Mia Hanover.

Now Mia probably had more money than all of those young women put together. But it meant nothing. She'd give every penny of it away to go back to being that poor Mia whose mother was still alive and cutting hair with not much skill, but a whole lot of love.

Blinking at the mist of tears that had gathered in her eyes, Mia quickly looked away from him and adjusted the pack on her back. "We'd better be going, don't you think?"

The abrupt change in her took Marshall by complete surprise. Moments ago she'd seemed eager to hear about his friends and then when he'd barely mentioned hers, she'd dropped a curtain and went off to someplace he wasn't invited.

For a moment he considered taking her by the shoulders and asking her point blank about her life, her past. But so far the day had gone so well that he didn't want to push his luck. There would come a time for him to gently pry at her closed doors and when that time arrived he would know it. Right now he was going to be content with her company.

For the next hour, as the two of them slowly made their way up the rough crags of the mountainside, Marshall tried to forget about the empty look he'd seen on Mia's face when he'd suggested she'd been a star attraction in high school. He didn't like to think that her past had been less than happy, but he wasn't blind. In a sense she was like Doris Phillips, who'd come to his office for help. She was putting on a brave pretense at happiness, but underneath her smiles there was a wealth of pain.

But what had caused it? Marshall wondered, as he hammered an anchor in between two slabs of rock. A man? With Mia's striking looks he'd be a fool to think a man hadn't been a serious part of her life at some point. Hell, for all he knew she could already have been married and divorced. That notion left such a bitter taste in Marshall's mouth that he felt almost sick.

With the last anchor in place, Marshall attached a strong rappelling rope and slipped it through a ring on his belt. In less than a minute, he'd swung himself down to the narrow ledge of rock where Mia was patiently waiting.

"I really think I've lost my mind. Are you sure I can do this, Marshall?"

Her question came as he girded a belt around her hips, then tested the buckle with a hard tug to make sure it was secure.

Straightening to his full height, he forced himself to rest his hands on his own hips rather than the sweet tempting curve of her behind. "We'll take the easiest route. Just remember everything I've taught you. And once you begin climbing, don't start staring down at the floor of the canyon. You might get vertigo and then we'd be in a hell of a mess."

"I don't get vertigo," she said with a frown. "See, I'm looking down now and nothing—"

Before she could get the remainder of her words out, she felt as though the top half of her was swaying forward. Frantic that she was about to tumble head over heels down the mountainside, she snatched a death grip on Marshall's arm.

He reacted instantly by snaring her with both arms and wrapping her tightly against his chest.

"Mia! Why did you do that?" he gently scolded as he cradled the top of her head beneath his chin. "If you'd lost your balance I might not have been able to catch you!"

Shivering with delayed fright, Mia clung to him and pressed her cheek against the rock hard safety of his chest. "I—I'm sorry, Marshall. I thought— I didn't think it would bother me. I've never been affected by heights before."

And Marshall had never been so affected by a woman before. It didn't matter that the two of them were precariously perched on a small shelf of mountain or that jagged edges of rocks were stabbing him in the back. All he could think about was covering her mouth with his; letting his hands explore the warm curves pressed against him.

"Oh, honey, don't scare me that way." Anguish jerked his head back and forth as unbearable images flashed through his head. "If you'd fallen, I would have had to jump after you."

Slowly her head tilted upward until her troubled gaze met his. "Don't say such things, Marshall. I'm—I'm not worth trying to save, much less dying for."

Softly, he pushed away the black strands of hair sticking to her damp cheek. "Why not? I wouldn't be worth much without you."

To Marshall's surprise tears suddenly gathered in her eyes and he could feel her trembling start anew, as though his words scared her even more than her near fall.

"Don't say something that serious, Marshall, unless you really mean it."

It suddenly struck him that he'd never been more serious. Losing Mia for any reason was something he couldn't contemplate.

"I couldn't be more serious, Mia."

Disbelief flashed across her face, but

Marshall didn't give her time to respond. Instead he gathered her chin between his thumb and forefinger, then lowered his head to hers.

"Don't argue with me, Mia," he murmured huskily. "Don't say anything. Just let me kiss you."

He could see questions shouting in her eyes, but her lips were silent, waiting to meet his. He groaned as a need he didn't quite understand twisted deep in his gut, then his eyes closed and his lips fastened hungrily over hers.

Chapter Ten

Two hours later, after climbing nearly to the timberline of the mountain, then descending back to their starting point, Mia and Marshall returned to the Jeep and were now traversing the rough track of road that would eventually carry them back to the resort.

Mia was hot, tired and thirsty. Her knees were scraped raw and she'd cut a painful gash in her palm, but those problems were minor discomforts compared to her spinning thoughts.

The kiss Marshall had given her on the rock ledge had frightened her with its intensity and she was still wondering what had been behind it and his suggestive words. He couldn't be getting serious about her. They'd only known each other a few days. On top of that, he wasn't a man who wanted to get serious about any woman. And even if he were, she was carrying a trunk full of baggage. All he had to do was open the lid to see she wasn't the sort of woman he'd want to gather to his heart.

"Are you too tired to stop by the meadow?" Marshall's voice interrupted her burdened thoughts and she glanced over to see he'd taken his eyes off the road and was directing them at her. Just looking at him pierced her with a longing that continued to stun her. She'd never expected to feel so much desire for any man. Even Lance, whom she'd believed that she'd once loved, had never elicited the hungry need she felt for Marshall. What did it all mean? And where could it possibly lead her, except straight to a crushed heart?

"I'm tired, but I did want to take a closer look at the flowers."

The corners of his lips turned softly upward. "Good," he said. "There's something I want to talk with you about before we get back to the resort."

Her brows lifted with curiosity, but she

didn't have time to ask him to explain further. By now the road had leveled and they were quickly approaching the flower-filled meadow.

Moments later Marshall parked the Jeep along the side of the road. As she waited for him to skirt around the vehicle to help her out, she made a feeble attempt to smooth her mussed hair. She was trying to do something about the dirt and blood caked on her palm when he jerked open the door.

"What's the matter?" he asked as she quickly closed her hand away from his sight.

"Uh—nothing. I just gouged my hand a little on a rock. I'll clean it up later, when I get back to my cabin."

With a frown of concern, he gestured for her to give him her hand. "I'm the doctor around here, remember. Let me see."

Mia was reluctant to let him treat her, even for a basic scratch. Something had happened to her when he'd kissed her up there on the mountain ledge. It was like he'd woken her sleeping libido and turned it into a hungry tigress. Letting him touch her, for any reason, was enough to send her up in flames. But she could hardly explain any of that, so there was nothing left for her to do but place her hand upon his palm.

"Mia!" he exclaimed as he gently probed at the deep gash. "Why didn't you tell me you'd hurt yourself? This is going to have to be cleaned. Otherwise the dirt might cause infection. It might even need a stitch or two. And you're going to need a tetanus shot. We need to go to the office where I have the equipment to deal with this."

With a nervous laugh, she swung her legs over the side of the bucket seat and pulled her hand from his grip. His gaze dropped instantly to her raw knees and he shook his head with misgiving.

"You look like you've met up with a grizzly bear and lost the fight. I'm sorry, Mia. When I asked you out this morning it wasn't with the intention of getting you hurt."

"I'm not hurt, doc. Just scraped a little. Now help me out. You can take care of my wounds later. After I take a look at the flowers."

Seeing he wasn't going to deter her, he took a firm hold on her arm and helped her to the ground.

"Don't even think about trying to get away from me," he told her as he guided her into the deep grass of the meadow. "I don't want any more cuts and bruises on you."

The two of them walked several yards into the

quiet meadow before they found a seat on a fallen log bleached white by years of harsh elements.

Mia sighed with pleasure as she looked around at the thousands of tiny pink and yellow blooms carpeting the surface of the meadow. "It's like a fairy-tale world," she said in a hushed voice. "I don't think I've ever seen anything so pretty."

"I have."

"You mean the pool of water you showed me up on the mountain? Well, it was beautiful," she admitted with another sigh. "But not as much as this."

Without warning, his hand came against her face and he turned her head so that she was facing him. Her heart jolted at the tender glow she found in his brown eyes.

"I'm not talking about the pool on the mountain," he murmured, "I'm talking about this."

His fingers brushed against her face, as though her cheek was a rose too delicate to touch. Mia couldn't stop the strong leap of her heart or the blush that crawled up her throat and onto her face.

"You're a terrible flatterer, Dr. Cates. I never know what will come out of your mouth."

The faint grin on his face was both wry and wistful. "I never know myself. Sometimes I get into trouble for saying what I'm thinking. And right now I'm thinking I'd like to lay you down in all these flowers and make love to you."

His admission shattered Mia's composure and for a moment all she could do was stare at him. Then suddenly she realized she had to get away from him, before she fell into his arms like a complete fool.

Quickly, she started to push herself up from the log, but he caught her by the arm and tugged her back beside him.

"We'd better go. Now!" she blurted sharply.

"Calm down, Mia. I'm not going to act on my words. I was simply telling you what I felt. Surely it isn't a surprise to you that I want to make love to you."

Mia slowly breathed in and out as she tried to still the rapid beating of her heart. She could have told him that it wasn't him she was afraid of, but rather herself. Yet to do that would only reveal that she was falling for him, that she wanted the very same thing he wanted—to make love to him in a bed of flowers.

Bending her head, she said in a thick voice, "You're right, Marshall. I'm not some innocent young woman. I'm twenty-six years old and I—I've had a man in my life. We were close for a long while—very close. And I...don't want to give myself to anyone like that again."

She looked up to see his brown eyes searching her face and she felt a little more of her resistance slip, a little more of the hidden Mia screaming to come to the surface.

"What happened? He wouldn't make a commitment?"

No, he'd gotten tired of her obsessive hunt for her mother, Mia thought. Tired of her putting their relationship on hold while she'd pored over names and telephone numbers, searched through stacks of birth records and driven miles to strange places with the mere hope that she'd find a lead. By the time she'd actually found Janelle and fell into her newfound fortune, her relationship with Lance had suffered greatly. Yet she'd thought, hoped, that having financial security would change everything for the better and that she and Lance could finally be happy, marry and start a family. But the money had only caused more of a wall between them. He'd walked away, but not before accusing her of being selfish and unfeeling. Dear God, he'd been right, she thought sickly. And that was the hardest part she'd had to live with.

Bitterness coated her tongue when she answered, "He made a commitment, but then… changed his mind."

Silence settled around them until the raucous screech of a hawk lifted Mia's gaze toward the blue sky. The predator was circling, searching for a weak and easy prey to wrap his talons around. Only the strong survived in this world, she thought sadly. And she wasn't strong. She'd been weak and needy enough to allow Janelle to get her hooks in her, to draw her away from Nina, the only mother she'd ever known.

"I'm sorry you had to go through that, Mia. But I can tell you why it happened."

Her nerves went on sudden alert as she dared to look at him. Did he know? Had he guessed at the terrible mistakes she'd made?

"You can?" she asked in a strained voice.

His smile was gentle, almost loving, and her hammering heart quieted to a hard but steady pound.

"Sure I can. Call it what you want. Fate or the hand of God. That thing you had with the other guy ended because you were supposed to wind up here—with me."

Hopeless tears poured into her heart until she was sure it was going to burst, but she carefully hid the pain behind a wan smile.

"Marshall, you're just so…"

When she couldn't finish, Marshall did it for her. "Sweet? Romantic? Yeah, I know," he said, his eyes twinkling. "I just can't help myself."

Sighing, she slipped off the log and bent down to pick a handful of delicate wildflowers. Marshall watched as she lifted the blossoms to her nose and wondered why the more he learned about her, the more he was growing to love her.

Love. Was that what it was? This endless need to see her face, hear her voice, have her beside him? He'd never felt like this before. Never felt so protective of a woman, so mindful of her feelings. He wanted more than just sex from her. He wanted to cradle her in his arms, wipe away the sadness from her eyes and cherish her for the rest of his life. If that was love then he'd fallen like a rock tossed into a river.

"My parents are having a little farewell dinner for my twin brothers this weekend," he said suddenly. "I'd like you to go with me."

She turned to stare at him and he could see doubts running rampant over her face. He wanted to reassure her with promises that he'd never hurt her, but he figured anything he might say right now would ring hollow. He was going to have to earn her trust. Show her that he wasn't the same sort of man that had changed his mind and walked away from her.

"Where is this dinner going to be?" she asked finally.

"At my parents' home."

As she chewed thoughtfully on her bottom lip, Marshall rose to his feet and laid a hand on her shoulder.

"Don't worry, Mia, it'll be a casual affair. And my parents are nice, laid-back people. You'll like them." He squeezed her shoulder. "And I know they'll like you."

Her eyes drifted up to his. "I'm not sure it would be a good idea."

"It would mean a lot to me," he said softly. "A whole lot."

She drew in a shaky breath and then a wobbly smile slowly spread across her lips. "All right, Marshall."

Leaning his head back, he gave a loud yip of joy.

That Saturday, as Marshall drove the two of them to the Cates homestead on the west edge of town, Mia continued to ask herself what in heck had possessed her to agree to this outing. Meeting a guy's parents was a serious thing.

Or, at least, it was where she came from. She
wasn't sure that Marshall meant anything significant by his invitation. But if by some odd
chance he did, then she was digging herself
into a deeper grave. She couldn't continue to
let Marshall believe she was simply a rich
young woman who'd been raised in a nice,
wealthy family. Yet to confess would only
mean the end of their time together. And her
hungry heart just wasn't ready for that yet.

The Cates home was a brick two-story structure set on five acres of a gently sloping
property dotted with large shade trees. A
wooden rail fence cordoned off a large front
yard landscaped with beds of blooming peren-
nials and neatly clipped shrubs. A concrete
drive led up to a double garage. Presently the
garage was closed and Marshall parked his
Jeep next to a white pickup truck with logos on
the doors that read Cates Construction—Built
to Your Needs.

As Marshall helped her out of the vehicle
Mia stared at the professionally done sign. "I
thought you said your brother's business was
called Cates International. That says Construction."

"That's another Cates," he said with a laugh.
"The pa of the herd. Dad's been in the building

business since he was a very young guy. Started out with his dad—my grandfather. Before the gold strike most of their business was over in the Bozeman area. The economy in Thunder Canyon was so slow that the city did well to build picnic tables for the town square. But now Dad and his employees can't keep up with all the contracts being thrown at them from a number of townsfolk. He thinks it's great, but Mom isn't so happy. For years now she's been planning for them to take a trip from coast to coast, but that's been postponed until Cates Construction catches up or the town goes bust."

"Marshall, quit dallying around and come in! We've all been waiting for you!"

Mia looked over her shoulder to see a middle-aged woman with chin-length pale blond hair standing on the small square of sheltered concrete that served as the front porch. She was dressed casually in tan slacks and a white sleeveless blouse. The warm smile on her face made Mia feel instantly welcome.

"Coming, Mom!" he yelled, then wrapping an arm around the back of Mia's waist, he urged her toward a wide sidewalk that bordered the front of the large house.

"You're a true doctor, son. Always late,"

Edie Cates fondly teased as Marshall guided Mia up the steps.

"I like to keep with tradition," he joked back, then quickly thrust Mia forward. "Mom, this is Mia Smith. She's a guest at the resort. And, Mia, this is my mother, Edie, the beautiful female of the bunch."

"The *only* female of the bunch," Edie said with a laugh.

"It's very nice to meet you, Mrs. Cates."

Expecting the woman to shake hands, Mia was surprised when she slung an arm around her shoulders and began leading her toward the door. "It's Edie, my dear. Don't make me feel any older than I already do with that *Mrs.* stuff. And I'll call you Mia, if that's okay with you."

"Of course," Mia told her. "And thank you for having me as a guest tonight."

"It's our pleasure," she said. She opened the door and ushered Mia inside while leaving Marshall to follow. "None of our sons have been brave enough to bring a girl home to meet us until now. Marshall has definitely treated his parents by inviting you."

Mia tossed a look of surprise at Marshall, but he merely winked and grinned.

Edie ushered them through a small foyer, a

formal sitting room, then on to a den where the rest of the Cates family was congregated in front of a large television. A major league baseball game was playing on the screen, but the sound was turned low, telling Mia that the four other Cates men had been doing more talking than watching.

Over the next few minutes Mia met Marshall's father, Frank, a tall, well-built man with salt and pepper hair and a jovial attitude that reminded her of Marshall. Mitchell, the second oldest son, was an attractive man with the same dark coloring as his brothers, but very quiet. Especially when she compared him to Matthew and Marlon, the young twins, who were continually telling animated stories and swapping playful swings at each other.

After all the introductions were over, Edie passed around soft drinks and Marshall directed Mia to take a seat at the end of a long couch. If anyone noticed that he tucked her into the crook of his arm, they didn't let on, but Mia was riveted by the warmth of his torso pressed against her side, the weight of his hand lingering on her upper arm.

He was treating her as though she were someone special in his life and he wanted his family to know it. The idea was a thrilling one to

Mia. Even though she knew this time with him couldn't last forever, she decided that this evening she was going to relish it. After all, leaving Thunder Canyon would come soon enough.

After a few minutes of light conversation and much bantering between the four brothers, Edie rose from her husband's side and announced she was heading to the kitchen to check on dinner. Wanting to feel useful, Mia instantly rose to her feet and offered to help.

"I can manage, Mia," Edie said. "But I'd love the company."

With a smile for Marshall, Mia quickly eased out of his gentle clasp and followed the woman out of the room and down a short hallway.

"Mmm, something smells delicious," she exclaimed as the two women pushed through a swinging door into the large, brightly lit kitchen.

"Lasagna. I hope you like Italian food. All the boys love it. Frank prefers steak, but since this is the twins' last night at home, he wants them to be treated."

"I love pasta of any sort," Mia told her as she watched the other woman open the oven door on a gas range and peer into the hot cavern.

"I do, too. And it shows in all the wrong places." Chuckling, she patted one shapely hip.

"I think you look beautiful," Mia said sincerely. "And you certainly don't look like you've had four children." Nor did she look as though she'd had the nips and tucks from a plastic surgeon that Janelle and thousands of other women chose to have in order to appear youthful.

Edie removed the large glass casserole dish full of bubbling lasagna and carefully placed it on the top of the stove. "You're very kind, dear. And very pretty. I can see why you caught Marshall's attention."

Feeling more than awkward, Mia let the woman's comment slide. "Is there anything I can do to help? Make a salad? Ice glasses?"

With a knowing chuckle, Edie glanced at her. "Don't want to talk about that, huh? Well, don't worry, I'm not a nosy mother. Now that the boys are grown, I stay out of their private lives unless I'm asked advice." She moved on down the counter and began to pull silverware from a drawer. "It's better that way. Otherwise they resent the interference." She laughed. "'Course there are times I'd like to tell them plenty."

Mia joined her at the cabinet counter. "I wish my mother were so understanding."

Edie glanced up from counting a handful of forks. "Does she live close to you?"

In the same house, but Mia wasn't going to admit that. It made her sound like a child who was now all grown up but too indolent to leave home. When actually the circumstances of living with Janelle were nothing close to that. Mia had fought against moving into the Josephson mansion. She'd wanted to keep her independence and privacy. But Janelle had played on Mia's soft heart by pointing out that she'd gone for twenty-five years believing her baby had died, surely living in the same house with her was not too much to ask. Not wanting to hurt her mother any more than she'd already been hurt, Mia had agreed and moved into the stately house. Ultimately that move had been a mistake, one that she was still paying for.

"Yes. And she can be very controlling. That's one of the reasons I've been vacationing here in Thunder Canyon," she admitted before she could stop herself. "Sometimes a person needs a little breathing room." She slanted a regretful glance at Marshall's mother. "That sounds pretty awful, doesn't it?"

Her expression empathetic, Edie reached over and touched Mia's arm. "No. It sounds perfectly human to me." She smiled warmly and with an ease that totally charmed Mia, she quickly changed the subject by pointing to a cabinet above her head. "Now if you'd like to ice the glasses, you'll find them there. Looks like there're seven of us tonight. A nice lucky number."

Midway through dinner it struck Mia that the Cates were the sort of family she'd always dreamed of being a part of. Marshall and his siblings were close enough to bicker and tease without fearing that their love for each other could ever be shaken. They had parents that still adored each other after decades of marriage. Obviously Edie and Frank had raised their four boys with love and that love had stood as an anchor for them as they'd grown into men. If either parent was the controlling, smothering sort, it wasn't evident to Mia. Of course, with a guest present, she assumed that everyone was probably on his or her best behavior. Still, as far as she could see, there were no taut undercurrents or furtive glances of impatience between family members. All Mia could see was genuine affection and it filled her heart with golden warmth, like a treasure chest spilling over with incomparable riches.

As the group dined on plates of lasagna accompanied by hunks of garlic bread, Mia drank in the easy ambiance like sips of wine to be savored. With Marshall at her side showering her with attention and affectionate glances, it was easy to let herself dream that she was home and she was loved.

"Did you make any extra lasagna, Mom?" Marlon asked as the meal began to wind down. "You know Matthew and I will need something to eat once we get to the dorm."

The roll of Edie's eyes was tempered with an indulgent smile. "I'm sure there's not a place on campus that sells food," she teased. "That's why I made an extra pan. When you get to your dorm room just make sure you keep it in the refrigerator. You can't leave it sitting out, then rake off the mold expecting it to be good."

Mia looked at Matthew, who was sitting directly across the table from her. Marlon was striving for a career in business agriculture while Matthew was working his way toward a law degree. Both twins appeared eager to head back to school, although she could sense they were going to miss being home. "When will you two be leaving?" she asked.

"In the morning," Marlon spoke up before his twin could answer. "As soon as I can kick Matthew out of bed."

"Hah!" Matthew tossed at his brother. "I'll

be the one doing the kicking. You don't even have your bags packed."

Marlon shot him a droll look. "That's because I'm not the dandy you are. I don't need trunks of clothing or hours to pack it. Five minutes to fill a duffle bag will be enough for me."

From the end of the table, Frank chuckled. "Well, I know one thing," he said to the twins. "Both of you are going to miss having your mom do your laundry and cooking."

Edie smiled at her two youngest sons, then settled a privately shared gaze on her husband. "Oh, Frank, you know I've spoiled the twins the same way I have you and Marshall and Mitchell. And just like you three, they take it all for granted. Once they get back to college, they'll forget all about their ole mom and everything I've done for them."

Both twins groaned with loud protest and everyone around the table began to laugh. Except Mia. She wasn't hearing the laughter or seeing the teasing faces. She was suddenly back in Denver and Nina Hanover was begging her to come home, which at that time had been a little apartment in Colorado Springs. Nina, a little drunk and full of a whole lot of pain, had accused Mia of forgetting her mother, the mother that had raised her from a newborn, the mother that had worked and sacrificed to keep a roof over Mia's head and food on their table.

The memories were suddenly too much for Mia to bear and, as tears began to blur her vision, she frantically realized she had to get away from the dinner table before she broke down completely.

"Please excuse me," she mumbled, then before Marshall or the rest of the family could respond in any way, she scraped back her chair and rushed from the room.

Chapter Eleven

Mia's abrupt departure from the dining room halted all laughter and Marshall stared in stunned silence at his parents and brothers.

"What happened?" Mitchell was the first one to ask. "Did somebody say something wrong?"

Edie looked across the table at Marshall who was already tossing down his napkin and rising to his feet. "Son, you'd better go see about her. I got a glance at Mia's face as she turned away from the table and I thought she looked sick. Dear heaven, I hope my cooking hasn't upset her stomach."

Marshall headed out of the dining room.

"Don't worry, Mom," he tossed over his shoulder. "I don't think it's anything like that. The rest of you finish dinner and I'll go check on her."

After checking the guest bathroom and finding the door open and the light off, Marshall hurried to the den. When he didn't spot her there, he stepped through a sliding back door and onto a small patio. During dinner, the sun had fallen and now golden-pink rays were slanted across the backyard.

At first glance he didn't notice the still figure standing with her back to him in the shadow of a poplar tree. But as he turned to step back into the house, a flash of her coral-colored blouse caught his eye.

Quickly, he made his way across the yard to where she was staring out at the ridge of nearby mountains. If she was aware of his approach, she didn't show it, even when he came up behind her and gently placed his hands on her shoulders.

Through the thin fabric of her blouse, he could feel her trembling and concern threaded his softly spoken words. "Mia. What are you doing out here? Everyone is worried."

Several moments passed and then she reached up and wiped at her eyes. The realization that she'd been crying hit him hard.

"I'm…sorry, Marshall," she said in a raw, husky voice. "I—didn't mean to upset your family. They've all been so wonderful to me. Too wonderful."

The painful cracks in her voice struck Marshall right in the heart and he slowly turned her to face him. Tears rimmed her beautiful eyes and spilled onto her cheeks. Marshall wiped them away with the palm of his hand.

"If everything is so wonderful then why are you out here crying?"

Bending her head, Mia stared at Marshall's boots. She'd gone and done it now, she realized. There was no way she could easily explain away her behavior. Not without giving away the past she desperately wanted to keep hidden. But he was expecting an explanation and she was so sick of the deception she'd been playing.

"I—uh—guess I just got swamped with memories, Marshall. Your family is so nice and I guess it hit me all over again that mine is gone."

"Gone?" he repeated blankly. "I remember you saying your father died long ago. Are you telling me that your mother has passed away, too?"

She lifted her gaze and the concern she saw

in Marshall's eyes gave her the strength to release the words bottled in her throat. "Yes. About a year ago. She—uh—was killed in an auto accident. And I—I've been having a hard time dealing with—the whole thing. I miss her terribly. Her death—" She paused, swallowed, then tried to keep her voice from breaking. "Her death has left a hole in me, Marshall, and I—just don't know how to fill it back up."

With a gentle shake of his head, he said, "I'm so sorry, sweetheart. I know that doesn't mean much, but I really don't know what else to say. If I told you that I understand what you're going through, I'd be lying. I've been blessed. I don't know what it's like to lose a loved one."

She blinked furiously at the fresh tears that threatened to spill onto her cheeks. "My parents were like yours, Marshall. They loved each other very much and they loved me— maybe more than I realized—until they were gone. It troubles me that I didn't appreciate them as much as I should have."

He reached out and smoothed a hand over the crown of her head. The soothing touch caused Mia's eyelashes to flutter down and rest against her cheeks. If only she could always have him by her side, she thought longingly. To soothe her when she hurt, to laugh with her when she was happy, to simply love her for who and what she was.

"We're all guilty of that, Mia. I hate to admit it but there have been plenty of times that I've taken my family for granted and forgotten to show them how much they mean to me. Fortunately they know that I love them anyway. I'm sure your parents knew that you loved them, too."

Over the past months Mia didn't think her heart could hurt anymore than it already had, but the pain ripping through the middle of her chest was so deep it practically stole her breath.

"I hope so," she choked out. "But it's different for me, Marshall. My family...well, I wasn't raised up like you."

"I never expected that you were," he countered. "Dad has always made a nice living for his wife and children, but I'm sure it can't compare to your family's wealth."

She shook her head viciously back and forth and the truth, or at least part of it, demanded to be let out. "No—you have it all wrong, Marshall. I wasn't born into wealth. Will, my father, raised potatoes and alfalfa hay and Nina, my mother, was a simple housewife. We lived in a modest farmhouse outside of the little town of Alamosa down in southern Colorado. We weren't rich—just rich in love. It's—" she paused long enough to draw in a deep breath and lift a beseeching gaze up to his "—it's taken me a long time to realize that, Marshall. Too long."

Marshall would be lying if he said that her admission hadn't taken him by surprise. Learning she wasn't a born heiress was the last thing he'd expected to hear. But her stunning declaration couldn't compare to the emotions piercing him from all directions. He'd never imagined that he could feel someone else's pain this deeply. It had emanated from her like a tangible thing and wrapped around his heart like an iron vice. And like a flash of lightning, Marshall suddenly realized he was just now learning what it truly meant to be a doctor to the needy and a man to the woman he loved.

"Oh, Mia. I'm glad you told me. And if you think it could make me care about you less, then you've got it all wrong. I don't care that you weren't born into wealth. None of that matters. All I want is for us to be together."

He *cared* about her? Dear God, maybe it didn't matter to him that she'd come from a modest background, Mia thought. But he couldn't begin to imagine the whole story. And he wouldn't be nearly so understanding if he found out she'd caused her mother to turn into a drunk driver. Nina Hanover had turned to a bottle of vodka to drown out her sorrows. First to forget that she'd lost her husband, then more heavily because her daughter had deserted her for a pile of riches. Or at least, that's the way it had seemed to Nina. Actually, Mia hadn't ignored her mother because she'd stopped loving her. She'd simply grown weary of dealing with Nina's drinking and whining and pleading. It had been easy to let Janelle shield her from all of that and give her a quiet haven away from Nina's emotional problems. But Mia couldn't forsake Nina entirely and one day she'd agreed to meet her for lunch. She'd had plans of talking her mother into entering rehab and finding the help she needed. But Nina had ended any and all of Mia's hope when she'd climbed behind the wheel of a car and crashed on her way to meet Mia.

"Marshall, I..." The rest of her confession lodged in her throat like pieces of poisoned bread. She couldn't tell him the rest. Not tonight. Maybe she was wrong, even greedy for not telling him everything. But she wanted this fairy-tale time with Marshall to keep going for as long as possible. "Thank you for under-standing," she finally whispered.

For long, expectant moments, his dark gaze gently skimmed her tear-stained face and then suddenly his head was bending down toward hers, blocking out the last bit of twilight.

When his lips settled over hers, she didn't even try to resist. The taste of his tender kiss was the very thing she needed to soothe her aching heart and before Mia realized what she was doing, she rose up on tiptoes and curled her arms around his neck.

Marshall was about to place his hands on her hips and draw her even tighter against him, but thankfully, before their embrace could turn into something more passionate, he caught the sound of footfall quickly approaching from behind.

With supreme effort, he quickly lifted his head and turned to see his mother watching them with a frown of concern.

"Sorry, I didn't mean to intrude," she quickly apologized. "We were all getting a little worried about Mia. Is everything all right?"

Clearing his throat, Marshall arched a questioning brow down at Mia. Of course *everything* wasn't okay with Mia, he realized sadly. It was going to take her a long time to recover from the recent loss of her mother. But at least for the moment her tears had dried and a wan smile was curving the corners of her lips.

Mia stepped toward Marshall's mother. "I'm fine, really, Edie. And I'm so sorry that I ruined the last of your dinner. Please forgive me. I guess—I got a little too emotional thinking about my own family."

Edie closed the short distance between them and wrapped Mia's hand in a warm clasp between the two of hers. "Don't bother yourself one minute over it. You didn't ruin anything. We've loved having you. Would you like to come back in now and have coffee? I'm afraid that the twins have already dug into the brownies, but there're plenty left."

Mia glanced back at Marshall and all he could think about was taking up their kiss exactly where they'd left off.

"I think Mia's had enough of the rowdy Cates brothers for one night," he told his mother. "If you and Dad won't mind, I'm going to take her home."

Edie's understanding smile encompassed both Mia and her son. "Of course we won't mind. As long as you two promise to come again soon."

"You can bet on it," Marshall told her, then

bent and placed a kiss on his mother's cheek. "Tell everyone goodbye for us, will you?"

"Sure."

Edie turned and disappeared through the patio doors. Marshall took Mia by the arm and led her around the house to where his Jeep was parked.

Before he opened the door to help her in, he gathered her back into his arms. Then resting his forehead against hers, he whispered, "I hope you don't mind that we're leaving. Do you?"

The suggestive tone in his voice set her heart thumping with anticipation. "No. I'm ready to go if you are."

He placed a quick, but promising kiss on her lips. "I couldn't be more ready."

Once they were in the Jeep driving back to the resort, Mia stared, dazed, out at the darkened landscape. Marshall had said he cared about her. He couldn't *love* her, she mentally argued. Could he? Especially now that he knew she wasn't a born-and-bred heiress.

She didn't realize he'd passed her cabin and had driven them on up the mountain to his house until the vehicle came to a final halt and she looked around her at the encroaching pine forest.

"This isn't my cabin, it's yours," she stated lamely. "What are we doing here?"

He shoved the gearshift into first and pulled the key from the ignition. "I didn't think you needed to be alone right now. And I wasn't sure you'd invite me in if we stopped at your place."

Her heart melting at the tender look on his face, she reached over and touched his hand with hers. "I was going to invite you in. But this is just as good."

Leaning toward her, he slipped a hand behind her neck and pulled her face toward his. His lips were warm and searching, inviting her to forget everything but him.

Mia was about to wriggle closer when Leroy's loud barks caused her to flinch away from him.

"Oh. Leroy scared me!" she exclaimed.

"Damn dog," Marshall muttered. "He has no timing at all."

"Yes, but he's a sweetheart," Mia crooned as she looked toward the front-yard gate. The dog was reared up on his hind legs, pawing eagerly at the wooden post where the latch was located.

Mia laughed and Marshall shot her a droll look. "Hey, beautiful, you're confused. I'm supposed to be the sweetheart around here. Not Leroy."

She was still laughing as they crossed the yard and entered the house with a happy Leroy trotting behind them. But the moment he shut the door and drew her into his arms, he swallowed up her chuckles with a kiss hot enough to curl her toes.

"I think Leroy is watching," she whispered when he finally lifted his lips a fraction from hers.

"Not for long."

She was trying to guess his intentions when he suddenly bent and scooped her up in his arms.

"Marshall!" she squeaked. "You're going to drop me!"

"Then you'd better hang on," he warned with a chuckle.

Flinging her arms around his neck, she clung to him tightly as he began to walk out of the living room. When his route took them down a narrow hallway it was obvious he was headed to a bedroom and she wasn't so naive that she had to ask why. For the past few days, she'd felt the two of them drawing closer and closer, ultimately leading them onto this path and this very moment.

Seconds later, Marshall entered a room, kicked the door shut behind them, then set her on the floor. Black shadows filled the corners and shrouded most of the furniture, while faint shafts of light sifted through the windows and slashed across part of the bed and the upper half of his face. The illumination was enough to give Mia a glimpse of his heated gaze and it arced into her like a sizzling arrow.

Her heart was suddenly pounding, pushing heated blood to every inch of her body as his hands came up to cradle her face.

"You can tell me you're not ready for this, you know," he whispered gently. "But I hope you are."

He was giving her the opportunity to walk away from him and the intimacy he was offering. He was giving her a moment to analyze her feelings and consider the consequences of making love with him. But Mia didn't need the extra moment to question the rightness or wrongness of being here. She was sick of analyzing and agonizing over every decision she made, tired of guarding her true feelings. She wanted to be a woman again and for tonight that was enough to justify stepping into his arms.

Slipping her arms around his waist, she rested her chin in the middle of his chest and tilted her face up to his. "I want you, Marshall. Here with you is the only place I want to be."

Groaning with a mixture of relief and need, he skimmed his hands down the sides of her arms. "I want you, too, baby. So much."

Her breath caught as his head slowly lowered down to hers and then she forgot all about breathing as his lips settled over hers and his hands clasped her waist and drew her against the length of his body.

Like a desert wildfire, his kiss raged through her body, turning her insides to molten mush. His tongue pushed its way past her pulsing lips and then she was lost, groaning with abandoned pleasure as he explored the dark cavern of her mouth, the rough edges of her teeth.

In a matter of moments a tight ache started somewhere deep within her and began to spiral outward and upward until she was twisting and clinging, fighting to find the relief his body would give her.

Fueled by her heated response, Marshall continued to kiss her as his hands quickly went to work releasing the buttons on her blouse and finding his way to the warm flesh beneath. Her skin was smooth beneath his fingers. He couldn't touch her enough as his hands slid upward, along the bumps of her ribs, then around to her spine where they climbed until his thumbs snared in the fastener on her bra.

With deft movements he unhooked a pair of eyelets and the garment fell apart, the loosened tails dangling against her back. He broke the kiss and their gazes locked as he slowly pushed the blouse from her shoulders, then slipped the straps of her bra down her arms.

Beneath the trail of his fingers, he could feel goose bumps breaking out along her skin, telling him just how much he was affecting her. As for him, he felt like an awkward teenager, touching a woman for the first time. His heart was pounding. Blood was rushing to his head, fogging his senses, filling his loins to the aching point. He'd never wanted so much. Needed so much.

He was asking himself what it could mean when the bra fell away from her breasts and the perfectly rounded orbs were exposed to his gaze. The lovely sight of puckered rose-brown nipples momentarily froze him and then slowly, seductively, he raked the pads of his thumbs across the delicate nubs.

Almost instantly Mia's head fell back. A moan vibrated in her throat. Bending his head, Marshall slid parted lips along the arch of her neck, over the angle of her shoulder, then lower until he was tasting the incredibly soft slope of her breasts.

When his mouth finally fastened over one taut nipple, Mia was panting, thrusting her fingers against his scalp, urging him.

When he finally lifted his head, he was shaking from the inside out and wondering if he was in some glorious dream that would end at any moment. But Mia's warm flesh brushing against his was enough to remind him that she was real and waiting to become his woman, his lover. The implication brought a tremble to his hands as he reached to undo the front of her jeans.

"Let me do this," she whispered as his fingers fumbled with the button at her waist. "It will be faster."

Not in any condition to argue with her, Marshall eased away from her and while he struggled to fling aside his own shirt and jeans, he darted hungry glances at Mia until she finally pushed the denim off her hips.

With his own clothes out of the way, he stood watching as she stepped from the pool of fabric. The sight of her plump breasts and tiny waist, the curves of her hips and the long firm muscles of her thighs just waiting for him to touch and taste was enough to leave him just short of speechless.

"Mia. Oh, Mia," he whispered.

Stepping forward he lifted her onto the queen-sized bed, then followed her onto the down comforter. As he enfolded her in his arms, she pressed her cheek against his and the sweetness of her gesture pierced his heart, filling it with something warm, something that had nothing to do with sex and everything to do with love. The idea scared him, but the feeling was so thrilling that he couldn't stop. Couldn't look back.

"Marshall, I didn't know how much I wanted this—you—until tonight. But when you kissed me out in your parents' yard...I don't know. Everything felt different—right. Does that make sense?"

At this moment nothing made sense to Marshall except the extraordinary need to kiss her, hold her, feel his body sliding into hers.

"Making sense doesn't matter," he said thickly. "You and me together—that's all that matters."

Rolling her onto her back, Marshall used the next few minutes to make a feast of the mounds and hollows of her body and each nibble, each tempting slide of his tongue sent shivers of longing down Mia's spine. In a matter of moments she forgot everything except the desire that was surging higher and higher, begging her body to connect with his.

When she began to moan and writhe beneath him, he eased back enough to slip the scanty piece of lace from her hips. The black triangle of hair springing from the juncture of her thighs beckoned his fingers. For a moment he teased the soft curls and then, lifting his gaze to hers, he stroked lower. Her eyes widened with surprise, then closed completely as he gently, coaxingly touched the intimate folds between her thighs.

"Marshall, Marshall," she said on a thick, guttural groan. "Don't torment me like this. I need—"

The rest of her words stopped on a gasp as one finger slipped into the moist heat of her body. Stock still, she waited, barely breathing as he stroked and explored that secret part of her. But after a few short moments the teasing rhythm of his movements was too much for her to bear.

Crying out with a mixture of intense pleasure and pain, she reached for the boxers riding low on his hips and, hooking her thumbs in the waistband, pulled them down around his thighs.

"Make love to me, Marshall. *Please.*"

The urgency of her whispered plea was like throwing accelerant on an already raging fire.

On the verge of losing all control, Marshall forced himself to move away from her and over to a chest of drawers where he fished out a small packet and quickly tore it open.

When he returned to her, Mia hardly had time to notice that he'd been dealing with protection. All at once his knee was parting her thighs and his hands were slipping beneath her buttocks, lifting her up to meet the thrust of his arousal.

A sudden rush of fiery sensations brought a keening moan to the back of Mia's throat and, seeking any sort of anchor she could find, her fingers latched a tight grip around his upper arms. Bending forward, he began to move inside her and when she slowly began to move with him, he brought his lips to hers and growled out her name.

"Mia. Mia. Touch me. Love me."

Happy to comply with his sweet request, she swept her palms over the hard muscles of his chest, down his ribs and abdomen, then back up until her fingertips lingered at his hard nipples.

With each bold foray of her hands, she heard his breath catch, felt his thrusts quicken. Frantic to keep pace with him, she wrapped her legs around his and clung to his sweat-drenched shoulders.

At some point the room around her spun

away, leaving a black velvety place where only she and Marshall existed. With each rapid plunge, he drove her to a higher ledge, where her heart was hammering out of control, her lungs burning with each raspy breath.

They took the climb together, racing frantically toward the peak of the mountain where a crescent moon poured silver dust and lit their pathway to the stars.

She was straining, her body screaming for relief, when Marshall's lips came down over hers to swallow up her cries and nudge them both over the last precipice of their journey. He drove into her like a man possessed, his hands and hips gripping her to him as he spilled his very heart into her.

His throaty groan of release launched Mia even higher and, like a rocket gathering steam, she shot straight through a bright, molten star. She cried his name as lights glittered behind her tightly closed eyelids. And then she was drifting, glowing, falling back to earth on a cloud of emotions.

When Marshall's senses finally returned, he was still breathing raggedly and sweat was rolling into his eyes and down his face. Beneath him Mia's body was damp and lax, her face covered with a tangle of black hair.

With a groan that sounded like it belonged to someone else, Marshall rolled to her side and reached to push the veil of hair away from her cheek. As his fingers brushed against her neck, he could feel her pulse hammering and he bent and pressed a kiss to the throb of her heartbeat.

"I'm not sure I'm alive," he murmured. "Are we in heaven?"

The corners of his lips tilted into dreamy smile. "I think I just went there."

Slipping a hand over her belly, he latched onto her hip bone, then rolled her onto her side and against the length of his body. After cuddling her head in the crook of his shoulder, he pillowed his jaw against the crown of her hair and closed his eyes in exhausted contentment.

For the first time in Marshall's life words seemed inadequate to describe what he'd just experienced. Joy was swimming around inside him, warming him like bright sunshine. Maybe that made him a sappy fool. But he didn't care.

"I knew it would be good with us," he murmured, then silently cursed himself for emitting such a stupid remark. Hell, good was a long way from portraying the connection he'd felt to Mia. Why couldn't he tell her that?

Because he was a chicken, he realized. Because even though she'd made love with him, his hold on her was still too fragile. Any remark suggesting a future together would send her running.

"Mmm. How did you know that? Experience?"

Sliding a finger beneath her chin, he tilted her face up to his, but the darkness of the room hid her expression. He touched the pad of his forefinger to the middle of her lips.

"Oh, Mia, I thought I knew what being with a woman was all about. But making love with you—" He shook his head, then chuckled with wry disbelief. "It felt like the first time. No—not the first time. The *only* time."

Her heart wincing with regret, she lifted her fingers to his face and slid them along the length of his jawline. "You'll feel differently about that in the light of day. Especially if you see me when I first wake up," she tried to tease.

His arms moved around her back and hugged her even closer. "I hope that means you're going to stay here with me tonight."

She was wondering how to best answer that question when his arms tightened around her even more.

"Don't bother answering," he said, "because

I'm not going to let you out of this bed for any reason. Except breakfast, maybe."

She tried not to let the possessive tone in his voice thrill her, but it did. Everything about the man thrilled her. And tonight she needed to be close to him, needed to let herself believe that she could be loved.

Bringing her lips up to his, she kissed him softly, temptingly. "Will you be doing the cooking?"

His sexy chuckle fanned across her face and curled her toes.

"Just tell me what you want."

Chapter Twelve

When Mia woke the next morning, she was momentarily startled by the strange room, but as she sat up in Marshall's bed, everything about the night before came rushing back to her. And the memories were enough to send a scarlet wave of heat across her face.

Oh, my, oh, my. She glanced at the empty spot where Marshall had lain beside her. Never had she behaved with such abandon. She'd responded to Marshall as though he'd been her lover for years rather than hours. Nothing had inhibited her. Nothing had stopped her from showing him how much she wanted him.

Well, she could be thankful she hadn't made a slip of the tongue and confessed that she loved him, she thought dryly, as she climbed from the bed and snatched up her clothing from the floor. At least she'd still have a shred of pride to hang on to whenever he eventually sent her packing.

Minutes later, after a quick shower in the private bath of his bedroom, she jerked on her jeans and blouse and hurried out to the kitchen. Marshall spotted her just as he was ending a call on his cell phone.

He snapped the instrument shut and hurried over to place a quick kiss on her lips.

"Good morning," she murmured shyly, then glanced at the phone he was dropping into pants pocket. It was six o'clock. She wouldn't expect him to be getting calls at this early hour. "Is anything wrong?"

He grimaced. "Afraid so. One of the guests is having some sort of chest pains. He thinks he pulled a muscle while rowing on the river yesterday. His wife is afraid it's his heart. I'm going to check him out. You can't be too careful with something like this." He glanced regretfully down at her. "There goes our breakfast for now. But I did have a chance to make coffee before the call came through. Why don't you have some and I'll be back as soon as I can. If I don't have a line of patients waiting on me, we could go to the Grubstake later for breakfast."

Mia quickly shook her head. "Don't worry about me. Go. Tend to your patient. That's the most important thing. I'll walk home to my cabin after I have a cup of coffee," she assured him.

Relief washed across his face. "You're too understanding, Mia." He planted another brief kiss on her lips, then turning to go, he tossed over his shoulder. "I'll see you later. This evening. Promise."

She waved him out the kitchen door and seconds later she heard the Jeep drive away.

Later that morning, after Marshall had determined that his early bird patient was suffering from a pulled ligament rather than a heart attack, he wrote the man instructions for care at home, along with a prescription for inflammation. The couple was just leaving his office when Ruthann arrived for work.

The redheaded nurse stared at Marshall as though the sight of him had sent her into shock. "What are you doing here?"

Marshall shot her a droll look. "I'm the

doctor around here, Ruthie, remember? Marshall Cates, M.D."

Rolling her eyes at him, she marched over to his desk and dropped a white sack full of sugary doughnuts and cream-filled pastries. "Shouldn't you add BS to that?"

He followed after her and snatched up the sack. As he pulled out a doughnut, he asked, "What does that mean?"

Ruthann banged the heel of her palm against the side of her head. "Do I have to spell it out for you? It's something you shovel out of the barn and you're full of it."

He bit off half the doughnut and swallowed it down after a few short chews. "Hell! That's not what I mean! Why are you insulting me by implying that I work banker's hours? I am a doctor," he reminded her pointedly. "I do have emergency calls."

Her brows shot up. "I thought you regulated those to Dr. Baxter."

"Not anymore."

"Since when?" she countered.

Frowning, he dropped into his desk chair and pulled another pastry from the sack. "Since a few days ago," he answered with a tinge of annoyance. "Since I decided I needed to do more around here to earn my pay."

Ruthann slapped a palm against her forehead and sank into a chair angled toward the front of Marshall's desk. "My God, let me sit down! I think I'm hallucinating—I think I'm actually seeing a doctor with a conscience."

He leveled a gaze at her. "Sometimes it stuns me that you can be such a mean woman."

She started to laugh and then another thought must have struck her because she frowned at him in confusion. "What was the emergency that called you out of your bed this morning?"

"Chest pains. But it was nothing serious. The patient and his wife were very relieved. And grateful. Made me feel good to help them. Even if I did have to miss cooking breakfast."

This time Ruthann did laugh, although the sound was more like a snort.

"Yeah. Sure, Marshall. You slave over the stove every morning, then eat a sack of pastries after you get to work."

Dusting the powdered sugar from his hands, he leaned back in the cushioned leather chair. He was exhausted. But it was the most pleasant sort of exhaustion he'd ever felt in his life. Mia had kissed him, touched him, whispered to him, turned him inside out with her lovemaking. He felt like a new and different man. And suddenly all the things he'd considered unimportant in life were now shouting at him to take a second look.

"Ruthie, do you think I'd make a good father?"

The startled nurse scooted to the edge of her chair. "Did you get drunk last night?"

Only on love, he thought. It was crazy. Foolish. He'd never imagined that the bug would bite him. He'd thought he was immune. But he felt like a grinning idiot and it was downright glorious.

"No. And I asked you a perfectly logical question," he shot at her.

She drew in a long breath and slowly released it. "Don't you think you ought to be a husband first?"

He pondered her question as he reached for another doughnut. "Yeah. That would be the way to do it, wouldn't it? A husband and then a father. Yeah. I could do it. Just follow after my dad."

"Well, I have to admit that Frank Cates is probably the best example of both. But as for you—you're thirty-four years old. You've gone through women like a stack of cotton socks. No," she said with a shake of her head, "if you had a wife you'd only end up breaking her heart and then I'd really hate you."

"I wouldn't do any such thing," he countered.

She snatched up the bakery sack before he could reach for the last pastry. "You're not only crazy this morning, you're eating like a hog. Why in heck are you so hungry?"

A wicked grin spread across his face. "Exercise, Ruthie. You ought to try it some time."

With a roll of her eyes, she left the room, carrying the last sugary treat with her.

Later that day, Mia sat on the porch of her cabin, trying to read, trying to forget the endless times Janelle had rung her cell phone today and, even more, trying to come to terms with the fact that she'd fallen in love with Marshall.

An objective friend would probably tell her that she was simply still glowing after a night of good sex. But Mia didn't have a close friend here on the resort to confide in. And even if she did, she wouldn't go along with that reasoning. Yes, being in Marshall's arms had given her a glimpse of ecstasy, but it hadn't just been sex. Not with her half of the partnership. The only reason she'd allowed him to carry her to his bed was the love that had been growing in her heart, building until she'd been unable to shut it down or hide it away.

Now what was she going to do about it? she wondered miserably.

Fool! There's nothing you can do about it. Marshall believes you're a sweet girl who unfortunately lost her parents. Once he gets the real picture of who you are, he'll turn his back and walk away.

Painful emotions knotted her throat and misted her eyes, making it impossible to read the open book on her lap. She was trying to compose herself and will the attack of hopelessness away when the sound of an approaching vehicle caught her attention and she looked up to see Marshall's Jeep braking to a halt next to her rental car.

Desperate to hide her turmoil from his perceptive gaze, she quickly dashed the back of her hand against her eyes and rose to her feet. By the time he'd jogged up on the porch to join her, she'd managed to plaster a bright smile on her face.

"Hello, doc."

His lips tilted into a sexy grin, he slid his arms around her and locked his hands at the back of her waist.

Mia's heart fluttered with happiness as he brought a soft, sweet kiss to her lips.

"Hello, beautiful," he murmured.

"My, that's a special greeting."

The grin on his lips deepened. "You're a special girl. My girl," he added softly.

Her heart winced at the sincerity in his voice. The idea that he was actually starting to care for her only made matters a thousand times worse. It would be wrong to lead him into a relationship that could go nowhere. Yet she wanted him so. Needed him so. Oh, God, help me, she silently prayed.

Dropping her gaze away from his twinkling eyes, she buried her cheek against the middle of his chest. "How did your emergency go this morning? I hope everything turned out okay."

"It did." He rubbed his chin against the top of her head. "The guy's heart checked out perfectly fine. He had a pulled ligament."

"That's good."

"Yeah. I'm just sorry it interrupted our breakfast together. That's one reason why I'm here. I thought I'd make up for it by taking you to the Grubstake for a quick bite. And then…"

His suggestive pause had her tilting her head back to look up at him. The sultry squint of his eyes told her he'd already planned a repeat of last night and Mia realized if she wanted to avoid an even bigger heartache, she'd turn tail and run. But she couldn't. Not when everything inside her was hungering to be back in his arms.

"Then what?" she softly prompted.

"We're going on a bike ride."

Her eyes widened. "A bike ride! Where?"

He chuckled at the surprise sweeping across her face. "Up the mountain from my house. Where we found Joey and his mother. I never got to show you my special spot up there. Are you up for it?"

At this moment she felt certain she could run for miles. As long as he was by her side.

Smiling, she eased out of his arms and picked up the book she'd left laying in her lawn chair. "Just let me change into some jeans. The last time I went up a mountain with you my knees were ground into hamburger meat."

Laughing, he followed her into the cabin.

Two hours later, after eating hearty sandwiches and fries at the Grubstake, Mia and Marshall rode up the mountain, two miles past the spot where they'd found Joey, then left their bikes at the side of the road to walk into the woods.

When they first ventured into the thick forest of tall aspens and fir trees, Mia expected a long steep hike over treacherous boulders, but it turned out to be more of an easy stroll along a lightly beaten path.

"Do other resort guests know about this place of yours?" she asked as she closely followed him through a stand of aspens.

"I doubt anyone else has ever found it. I've never seen anyone else climbing up this far."

"Hmm. Well, no one else is a mountain goat like you are," she teased.

"Just wait. You'll see that this trip was worth it."

Moments later they rounded another stand of trees and suddenly an open area appeared before them and Mia gasped with shocked pleasure.

There before them were slabs of red rock towering at least fifty feet above their heads. Water was spilling over the top of the ledge, falling and tinkling against the rocks until it reached a natural pool edged with tall reeds and blooming water lilies. The spot was so incredibly beautiful that it seemed more fairy tale than real.

Mia's first instinct was to rush forward to get an even closer look, but before either of them took a step, Marshall grabbed her arm and silently pointed to a mule deer with a fawn at its side slipping quietly from the trees and over to the pool's edge.

As mother and baby drank, Mia looked up at Marshall and smiled gratefully. "Thank you for bringing me here," she silently mouthed up at him, so as not to give away their presence and startle the animals.

Marshall responded by bending his head and pressing his lips to hers. The kiss was full of tenderness and something else that Mia had never felt before. It tugged at her heart and filled her chest with such emotion that she could scarcely breathe.

When he finally lifted his head, they both turned their heads to see that the doe and fawn had disappeared. Marshall slipped his arm against her back and urged her toward the waterfall.

"Come on," he said quietly. "Let me show you where I come when I really want to think."

When they returned to Marshall's log house later that evening it was no surprise to Mia that the two of them ended up in his bed. Nor was it a surprise that their lovemaking was even more earthshaking for her than it had been the night before. Her heart was well and truly entangled with the man and each time she'd given her body to him, her very soul had gone with it.

This morning after cooking her a leisurely breakfast, he'd dropped her off at her cabin on his way to work. He'd kissed her goodbye with the promise of calling her later in the day to talk over plans of getting together tonight.

Since that time, Mia had been prowling around her cabin, unable to relax, unable to concentrate on anything except this impossible situation she'd fallen into.

Situation. No, it was far worse than a situation. It was a complete and utter disaster. This thing between them was snowballing, racing along so quickly that she didn't know how to put on the brakes, much less stop it. But stop it she had to. Now. Tonight. Before Marshall found out she was really Nina Hanover.

The ring of her cell phone interrupted her pacing and for a moment she simply stared in dread at the instrument. If Marshall was calling what was she going to say? Just enough to put him off without alerting him that something was wrong? Yes, she thought, frantically. If she had tonight alone, then maybe she could figure out how she was going to deal with him tomorrow.

For once she wished that the caller actually was Janelle. But the ID number glaring up at her was Marshall's and she was forced to answer. Otherwise, he'd wind up on her porch and she wouldn't be able to find the resistance to stay out of his arms.

Swallowing hard, she pushed the talk button and spoke. "Hi, Marshall."

"Hi, darlin'. I'm five minutes away from leaving the office. Tell me where you'd like to eat dinner. How about driving over to Bozeman? I doubt you've been off the resort since you first arrived."

It was true. Once Mia had decided to temporarily settle at Thunder Canyon Resort, she'd ventured no farther than town. She'd not wanted to show her face on any of the major cities along the interstate, just in case Janelle had private investigators out looking for her. And there was little doubt in Mia's mind that the woman had been searching for her. Since finding Mia's note explaining that she was taking an extended trip to give herself time to think, Janelle had probably whipped into action, doling out money to anyone who'd make a concentrated effort to find her runaway daughter.

"Uh—no, I haven't been to Bozeman." Her voice sounded strained even to her own ears, but she couldn't help it. Her heart was breaking and all she really wanted to do was throw down the phone and sob until she couldn't shed another tear.

"Is something wrong, Mia? You sound strange."

She swallowed again as her throat clogged with a ball of guilt and regret. "I—well, actually there is something wrong. My head. I—developed a migraine this afternoon. And it's really cracking. I don't think I can make it out of bed."

"Mia, honey! You should have called my office earlier! I can prescribe you something for the pain or if necessary give you an injection. Just hold on. I'll be there in five minutes."

"No!" she blurted, then realizing how frantic that sounded, she added, "I mean, there's no need for you to come over. I took something a few minutes ago and I'm going to try to sleep."

Several moments passed before he finally replied. Mia got the feeling that this sudden change in plans had really taken him aback. Well, it had done more than that to her. The pain that had started in her chest was now radiating through her whole body, leaving her numb and dazed. If there was some sort of painkiller that could wipe out this love she felt for him, then she desperately needed it.

"All right, Mia. But I'd feel much better if you'd let me examine you."

"Don't be silly, Marshall. It's just a headache. I'll be fine tomorrow. I'll call you then."

She could hear him drawing in a rough breath. The sound brought tears to her eyes and she swiftly squeezed them shut.

"I—I was really planning on us being together tonight," he said softly. "The house is going to be damn hollow without you."

She was choking, dying from the bitter loss washing over her. "I'm—sorry, Marshall," she spoke through a veil of tears. "I didn't want the evening to end like this, either."

"You can't help it if you're sick, honey. Try to get some sleep and I'll check on you in the morning."

Relieved that he'd accepted her excuse, Mia quickly told him goodbye. But once she'd pushed the button to end the call, she broke into racking sobs that continued until she'd cried herself to sleep on the sofa.

When Mia woke the next morning, her heart was so heavy she could hardly push herself into the kitchen to make coffee. For all she noticed, the bright sunshine pounding against the windowpanes of the cabin might as well have been fierce raindrops. The first real joy she'd found since Nina passed away was over.

The first real love she'd ever felt for a man couldn't be continued. She couldn't hold on to the happiness that love should bring to a young woman's life. And all because she'd made horrible choices in the past. Choices that painted her as a selfish gold-digger and someone that a good man like Marshall could never love.

After a quick cup of coffee, Mia decided the best thing she could do this morning would be to leave the cabin and go for a walk in the forest. That way when Marshall called or dropped by to check on her, she'd be gone. It was a cowardly way for her to behave, but she wasn't sure she could face him just yet without breaking down in tears.

She had changed into clean jeans and a white peasant blouse and was walking swiftly away from the cabin when she heard a vehicle approaching her from behind.

Her whole body heavy with dread, she turned to see Marshall's Jeep bearing down on her. He skidded to a stop beside her and hopped out with the athletic ease she'd come to associate with him.

"Good morning," she greeted, tilting her chin, bracing herself for what had to be.

"Good morning, yourself," he said, his

stunned gaze whipping over her face. "What are you doing out here? I thought you were sick?"

Her heart was pounding so hard she thought she might lose her coffee right there in front of him. "I—was going out for a little hike this morning."

"After being bedridden with a migraine? Don't you think that's a little much?"

Of course he would view it that way. He was a doctor. Oh, God, help her, she prayed.

Clearing her throat, she glanced away from him and continued to pray for strength. "Okay, Marshall. I confess. I didn't really have a headache last night. I…knew if I didn't tell you something like that…you would…well, the two of us would end up in bed together again."

Looking even more stunned, he closed the distance between them and put a hand on her arm. The contact sent shivers of excitement and aching regret through her rigid body.

Bemused, he shook his head. "I don't understand, Mia. I thought you *wanted* us to be together—to make love."

Tightening her jaw to prevent her lips from trembling, she said, "I did. But I've been thinking it all through. And I— Well, this thing between us is going too fast. Way too fast." She forced herself to look at him and quickly wished she hadn't. Pain was clouding his brown eyes and the idea that she'd put it there made her even sicker. "I believe that we...need to cool things between us for a while."

He sucked in a deep breath then slowly blew it out and as he did, his eyes narrowed to two angry slits. "Why don't you just come out and say what you really mean, Mia. You jumped into bed with me. You've had your fun. And now you want out. Well, it looks like I was wrong about you. Dead wrong."

She froze inside. "What do you mean?" she asked tightly.

His face like a piece of granite, he said, "I didn't believe you were just one of those rich little teases out for your own enjoyment. I thought you were different—sincere. But it looks like the joke is on me, isn't it? I've got to admit, Mia, you really had me fooled. I thought— Oh, to hell with what I thought. You obviously don't give a damn what I think anyway!"

He turned and climbed back into his Jeep and though everything inside Mia was screaming at her to call him back, to explain that she hadn't been teasing him, using him, all she could do was stand there, her gaze frozen on the vehicle as he drove away.

Once his Jeep rounded a stand of trees and disappeared from view, finality set in and washed over her heart like a crushing wave. Everything between them was over. She'd accomplished what she'd set out to do. Now all she had to do was get over the only love of her life.

Chapter Thirteen

Two days later the weather turned wet and unusually cool for late August. For the most part, the guests at the resort were whiling away their time with indoor games and rounds of warm drinks from the bar and the coffee shop.

Marshall's patients had dwindled down to none and by late afternoon, he told Ruthie to close up shop and let the answering service deal with any oncoming calls. The idle day was driving him crazy. With too much time to dwell on Mia, his office felt like a cage.

He left the building by way of the back

entrance and once in his Jeep, automatically turned the vehicle toward his home. But halfway there, he muttered a disgusted curse and made a U-turn in the middle of the dirt road.

There was no use in going home. The place was hauntingly empty without Mia.

That's what you get, Marshall, for letting the woman get close, for letting her into your home as though she were someone who'd be around for the rest of your life.

The accusing voice in his head was right. He'd been a fool to think an heiress would fit into his life on a permanent basis. What the hell had he been thinking? He hadn't been thinking. He'd been feeling. Only feeling.

Moments later, he passed the turn off to Mia's cabin and continued barreling on out of the resort. He'd not tried to contact her since their brief encounter the other morning. He wasn't a glutton for self-punishment and though he'd finally let his guard down and allowed a woman to get under his skin, that didn't mean he was a naive fool. She'd made it clear that she wanted to end things between them. There wasn't any sense in going back for more pain, to give her another chance to pour salt into his wounds.

By the time he reached town, he realized his misery was leading him to the one person he could really talk to. At this hour of the day, his brother Mitchell would be at work, but he wouldn't mind if Marshall showed up unexpectedly. With all of the Cates, family always came first.

Cates International, Mitchell's successful company, was located on the edge of town. The large metal warehouse's light green exterior was trimmed in a darker green and surrounded by a huge paved parking lot that was partially filled with displays of planting and harvesting equipment.

A fancy showroom was attached to one side of the building, along with Mitch's luxurious office, but Marshall ignored the double glass door entrance gilded with gold lettering and walked on to a simple side door that accessed the warehouse. If he wasn't swamped with customers, Mitch would most likely be inside, tinkering around in his workshop.

Having guessed correctly, Marshall found his brother working at a computer and from the look of deep concentration on his face he was in his creative mood.

Walking around the desk, Marshall stood behind his brother and peered over his shoulder. "Is that some new design you're drafting, or are you just trying to draw an ice cream cone?"

His concentration broken, Mitchell looked over his shoulder. "Hey, brother. What's up?"

Unable to summon a smile to his face, Marshall shrugged. "Nothing. The weather has everybody on the resort playing safely inside. I don't have a thing to do. And I thought…I'd come out and see what you're up to."

Mitchell pointed to the small object on the computer screen. "Nothing much, just working on a little toy that might eventually make me millions."

"What the hell is that? Looks like a dunce cap for a mouse."

Mitchell grimaced. "That's why you're the doctor and I'm the inventor. I'm trying to come up with a seed broadcaster that will work on a smaller implement but cover more ground. It would save hours of labor and gallons of diesel for farmers."

"Good luck. It might be nice to have one millionaire in the family," he said dryly.

Mitchell turned off the computer and rose to his feet, motioning for Marshall to follow him over to a little nook in the room where a coffee machine was located.

"You look like you need something to perk you up, big brother. I don't think I've ever seen you looking so grim."

Mitchell poured two cups full of coffee and handed one of them to Marshall. "I'd offer you a sandwich to go with it, but the crew ate them all."

"No matter. I'm not hungry," Marshall told him. "And I should leave. I'm interrupting your work."

Shaking his head, Mitchell walked over to a comfortable couch. After taking a seat, he patted the empty cushion next to him. "I needed a break anyway. Come on. Sit. I can see something is on your mind. Tell me about it."

Raking a weary hand through his windblown hair, Marshall took a seat. "I always thought the big brother was supposed to be the listener. I'm the big brother."

Mitchell grinned at that observation. "Then who's supposed to listen to you?"

Marshall lifted his gaze to the ceiling far above them. His brother was smart, successful and smart enough to avoid the snaring arms of a woman. Too bad he hadn't been more like Mitchell, he thought. Instead, he'd gone through women like a stack of cotton socks. Just as Ruthie had said. Only this time, the tables had turned and he was the one doing the hurting. Maybe he deserved this misery.

"I don't know. Dad, I suppose. But I can't talk to him about this. He'd only remind me that I'd wasted years of my life regarding women as playthings when I should have been looking for a wife."

Sudden dawning crossed Mitchell's face. "Ah. A woman. So that's what this mopey look of yours is all about. I should have known. So the heiress has dumped you already?"

Marshall glared at him. "You don't have to be so flip about it."

This time Mitchell frowned. "Well, what do you expect, brother? The woman isn't your style. I don't know why you're bothering with her anyway."

His jaw tightened and then he answered in a low voice, "Maybe because I loved her. Because I...still love her."

Mitchell was suddenly regarding him in a different light. "I've never heard you talk this way. You're scaring me."

"I'm scaring myself. Especially now that Mia doesn't want to see me anymore."

"Why?"

Bending his head, Marshall stared at the concrete floor. "How the hell should I know!

One day she was all warm and loving and the next she says she thinks we should cool it. I can't figure what's going on with her."

Mitchell studied him thoughtfully. "Hmm. Well, she seemed nice enough at the family dinner. A little introverted, but nice."

His heart was suddenly aching as he recalled the tears on Mia's face as she'd talked about losing her mother. He'd wanted so much to help her and he'd thought loving her would give her the support she needed. He'd been wrong. Painfully wrong. "She has reason to be. She's lost her family—her mother more recently."

Mitchell blew out a long breath. "Forget her, Marshall. She's trouble. You don't need a woman carrying around a trunk of emotional issues. Put Mia Smith out of your mind and find someone new."

Marshall groaned with frustration. "I don't want another woman, Mitch. I want Mia. That's the whole problem."

Mitchell laid a comforting hand on his brother's shoulder. "If that's the way you feel, then my advice is to go confront her. Make her tell you what's wrong."

Marshall regarded his brother for a long thoughtful moment before he finally gave him a jerky nod. "You're right. If Mia wants to dump me, she's going to have to tell me why."

At the same time Marshall was visiting with his brother, Mia had finally ventured out of the cabin and walked over to the lodge. The cold weather had made the past two days even gloomier for her and though she didn't want to risk running into Marshall, she couldn't continue to hide in her cabin. She had two choices, she thought grimly, face him with the truth or leave Thunder Canyon once and for all. Either way, she was bound to lose him.

Thankfully, there was a cheery fire burning in the enormous rock fireplace in the lounge and several guests were sitting around reading, talking and playing board games. Mia purchased a cup of hot cocoa from the coffee shop and carried it over to one of the couches facing the crackling flames.

She'd just made herself comfortable and was sipping at her drink when she looked around to see Lizbeth Stanton, the lounge bartender, easing down on the cushion next to her.

"Hi," she said. "Mind if I sit down?"

Since the woman was already sitting, the question seemed inane. Mia shrugged, while wondering what could have prompted Lizbeth to join her. Even though she was acquainted with the sexy bartender and had chatted with her during her stay here at the resort, the two of them weren't what you'd called bosom buddies.

"Not at all. Are you on a break from the bar?"

Lizbeth shook her head. "No. I don't go on for another thirty minutes. I saw you sitting here and thought I'd stop by. I—uh, there's something I've been wanting to say to you and you're probably going to take offense at my being so frank, but I don't know of any other way to approach you about this."

Piqued with curiosity now, Mia turned slightly toward the bartender. "Oh?"

Frowning prettily, the auburn-haired siren folded her arms against her breasts. "Yeah. I think you're making a big mistake. No, more like a *huge* mistake. Marshall is a great guy. Everyone around Thunder Canyon will tell you so. I don't know what your game is, but he doesn't deserve to be dumped."

Mia stiffened. Is that what all of Marshall's friends here on the resort were thinking? God, she couldn't bear it. "Where did you hear such a thing—that I dumped Marshall?"

"That's not important. News travels fast here

on the resort. Although all of his friends didn't have to ask what happened. They can see he's miserable thanks to you." Her accusing gaze was practically boring into Mia's eyes. "It's beyond me how any woman could throw away a man like Marshall. But you seem to be doing it quite easily."

Mia drew in a bracing breath and tried to remember she was supposed to be an heiress with class and manners. She couldn't fire back at the bartender. She couldn't scream out that good men like her father died and left grieving widows and lost daughters. That there were no guarantees for lasting love.

"Look, Lizbeth, I think you're making a mistake by putting Marshall, or any man for that matter, on a pedestal. They're fallible. They don't always stick around. Or haven't you noticed?"

Lizbeth sneered. "What's the matter with you anyway? Are you jealous because Marshall dated me first?"

As Mia looked at her in stunned disbelief, she suddenly realized that her stay here at Thunder Canyon Resort was well and truly over. Tonight she would pack and in the morning she would put Marshall and his friends behind her.

"No. Marshall doesn't belong to me."

Lizbeth rolled her eyes. "Can't you see that Marshall is crazy about you?"

Maybe he was in love with her right now, Mia thought painfully. But if he ever met Mia Hanover that love would dissolve like a sugar cube tossed into a cup of hot coffee. Swallowing away the burning tears in her throat, Mia muttered, "Marshall never has been a one-woman man. I think you know that, Lizbeth. Most love doesn't last forever and a woman needs to learn to lean on herself and cope with life on her own."

Pity suddenly filled Lizbeth's eyes. "You know, I think I'm actually starting to feel sorry for you. You're lacking something in here."

Lizbeth pressed fingertips to her heart and it was all Mia could do to keep from bursting into tears. Apparently this woman hadn't watched her father die. Hadn't watched her mother fall apart and turn to alcohol because she'd lost the love of her life. Mia wasn't blind or crazy; she understood that Lizbeth saw her as a hard-hearted woman.

Oh, if only that were true, Mia thought. If only her heart were made of steel, or anything that couldn't ache. Then walking away from Marshall wouldn't be tearing her apart.

Rising to her feet, she stared down at Lizbeth. "You're probably right," she said coldly. "You're a far better woman to nurse Marshall's wounds. Maybe with all your virtues you'll be able to persuade him to walk down the aisle with you!"

By the time Mia reached the last words her voice had risen to a trembling shriek. She sensed the guests around them were all turning their heads to take notice, but for once she didn't care. She raced out of the lounge and didn't stop running until she was completely away from the lodge and halfway to her cabin.

Two hours later, her bed was covered with open suitcases and she was blindly but methodically filling them with all her belongings.

The tears that had threatened to pour from her during her confrontation with Lizbeth had flowed like a river once she'd reached her cabin, but now they were dried tracks upon her cheeks. She felt dead inside.

She was pulling the zipper closed on a leather duffle bag when a knock sounded on the front door of the cabin. Frozen by the unexpected sound, she stared at the open door of her bedroom. Could that be Lizbeth wanting to go another round? If so, she was going to use a few choice words to send the woman on her way.

Leaving the bag, she walked out to the living room and peered through the peephole on the door. The moment she spotted Marshall standing on the other side, her heart stopped as though all the blood had drained from it.

He must have heard her approaching footsteps because he suddenly shouted through the door, "Mia, it's me. Let me in. I'm not going away until you do."

Marshall. In her wildest dreams she'd never expected him to speak to her again. Why was he here? To tell her that he didn't appreciate everyone on the resort knowing that she'd embarrassed and demeaned him?

Her hand trembling almost violently, she pushed back the bolt and opened the door. He didn't bother with a greeting or invitation. Instead, he strode across the threshold and came to a stop in the middle of the room.

Mia shut the door behind her and forced herself to turn and face him. He was dressed casually in jeans and boots and a navy-blue hooded sweatshirt. His cheeks were burnished to a ruddy color from the cool wind and his coffee-brown hair was tousled across his forehead. He looked so handsome, so endearing that it was all she could do to keep from running to him and flinging herself against his broad chest.

"I—" She swallowed hard and tried again. "I—never expected to see you here."

Anguish twisted his lips. "What were you thinking, Mia? That I'd simply keep my distance? Let everything between us end as though it had never happened at all?"

Fear rippled through her, making her insides quiver. She turned her back to him and bit down hard on her lip. "It would have been better if you had," she whispered starkly. "I'm a person that you need to forget, Marshall. I'm—no good. Not for you."

"What are you talking about?" he muttered roughly.

"Haven't you talked to Lizbeth?"

He walked up behind her but stopped short of putting his hands on her shoulders.

"No. What about Lizbeth? Has she been saying things about me to you?"

Mia bent her head, then shook it. "Don't worry. Only that you're Dr. Perfect and I'm stupid for throwing you away."

Moments passed in silence and to Mia's complete horror she felt more tears rush to her eyes. Dear God, where was this endless waterworks coming from? Why couldn't she gather herself together and stop her tears once and for all?

"Is that what you're doing?" he asked quietly. "Throwing me away?"

She squeezed her eyes, yet she couldn't hide the raw emotion in her voice. "No," she whispered. "I—I'm leaving…for your own sake."

Quickly, before he could stop her, she stepped around him and raced to the bedroom. Once there, she frantically began slinging the last of her clothes into an open suitcase.

Marshall hurried after her. "Mia? What—"

Glancing to see he'd followed her into the bedroom, she cried at him, "Don't try to stop me, Marshall! Don't ask me anything! It's useless. Totally useless!"

She was lashing out at him like a frightened kitten; hissing and pawing, when all she really wanted was to curl up in his arms.

Sensing that nothing was really as it had first seemed, Marshall went to her and folded his fingers around her shoulders. "Nothing is useless. Not when you love someone, Mia. And I love you. Don't you understand? Don't you care?"

I love you. How many times had she dreamed of hearing Marshall say those words to her? Too many. And now she had to rip them all away, to smear and mar the most precious thing he could possibly give her.

"I care. More than you could ever dream, Marshall. But—"

His hands came up to tenderly cup her tear-stained face and as the warmth of his fingers flooded through her, she suddenly realized she couldn't pretend anymore. Not with him. Not with anyone.

"Then what is it? Tell me," he softly urged.

She drew in a shaky breath, but it did little to brace her composure.

"I'm a phony, Marshall. I'm not really Mia Smith. I'm Mia Hanover. I—I've been using the name Smith in order to keep someone from trailing me."

Stunned, he dropped his hands from her face and she used the opportunity to turn away from his searching gaze.

"Someone," he repeated blankly. "Someone like a man? A lover? A stalker?"

With a shake of her head, she slowing began folding the last pieces of clothing lying atop the mounded suitcase.

"No, the only man I've ever been seriously involved with was so disgusted with me he left—walked away. He didn't care enough to come after me and try again. This person is a woman. She's—uh—my birth mother. Her name is Janelle Josephson."

Marshall looked confused. "You said your mother was killed in a car accident."

"That's right. Nina Hanover. She was my adoptive mother. She's the one who raised me since I was a baby, the one who nurtured me as I grew up, sacrificed to give me food, clothing and a roof over my head." Groaning with pain, she squeezed the fragile silk blouse in her hands. "You see, Marshall, when my father—my adoptive father—died, I was about to enter college. Up until then my family—my *life*—had been so nice. My parents loved me and although we didn't have lots of money, I had all the necessities. Daddy saw to that. But then he developed lung cancer and it seemed to take him almost overnight. Mom—Nina—was devastated. For more than twenty years, he'd been her whole life, the only man she'd ever loved. Losing him so suddenly broke her, Marshall. She couldn't deal with the grief and at some point—I can't even remember exactly when— she started drinking."

Marshall's head swung back and forth with complete dismay. "Oh, Mia. I'm so sorry."

"You won't say that. Not when I tell you the rest."

Putting a hand on her arm, he slowly turned

her back to him. "Mia, nothing you say will change my love for you. Believe that."

As she met his loving gaze a sob choked her to the point that she could scarcely get any words past her throat. "You don't understand, Marshall. I caused my mother's death! I caused Nina to get behind the wheel of her car and drive. She was driving to see me—to meet with me because...because I'd been avoiding her—moving on with a life away from her."

Marshall didn't make any sort of reply. Instead he cleared an area on the side of the bed and sat Mia down, easing himself down next to her. "I want you to slow down, Mia," he said gently. "Tell me what happened from the very start."

She wiped a shaky hand over her face and sniffed back her tears. "Maybe I'd better go back to after my father died. That's when everything started going downhill."

Nodding, he reached for her hand and clasped it tightly. "Your father died and your mother started to drink. Did she become an alcoholic then?"

Mia considered his question for a moment, then shook her head. "No. I don't think she was dependent on the stuff at that time. She didn't have the opportunity to drink too much, she was always working. But no matter how many jobs she had, we could barely afford rent and utilities."

"What about the farm? You didn't try to keep it?"

Regret twisted her features. "We were forced to sell it to pay off the astronomical medical bills. There wasn't much left after that and it went quickly. During that time I began to think that if Mom and I only had money it would fix everything. It would make her happy. She wouldn't have to work all the time and it would give us both security and all the things we needed. She wouldn't want to drink anymore and everything would be wonderful again. I thought it was the answer for everything. And then I began to wonder about my real mother. I kept thinking that if I could only find her she might want to help me."

The desperate picture she was painting struck Marshall like the blade of a knife. It was so far removed from the born-into-riches-heiress he'd first believed her to be and he could only wonder at the suffering she'd gone through.

"You didn't know the circumstances of your birth?"

Shaking her head, she looked down at his

hand closed tightly over hers. "No. Not a clue. Nina didn't know, either. And she didn't want me to know. She feared that if I did find my birth mother I might learn something that would haunt me for the rest of my life. But I wouldn't listen. The image of finding my birth mother had become a beautiful dream to me. One that I wasn't about to let go."

"How on earth did you find her? Adoption information is carefully guarded."

"It took years. I used the Internet and newspapers to ask questions and put out information. I met with any- and everyone associated with my parents back around the time I was born and tried to gather any sort of leads from what they recalled about my adoption."

"Were any of them able to help you?"

"In a roundabout way," Mia answered. "One man who'd lived next to our farm, but later moved from the area, remembered that my parents had traveled up to Denver to get me. And he thought that was where the adoption had taken place. With that information, it was logical to assume the records would be there and I was determined to get my hands on them somehow. But that was like butting my head against a brick wall. I begged, cajoled, even tried to con my way into getting a glimpse at my adoption papers. Security eventually threatened to have me arrested if I didn't quit badgering the filing clerks. Then I finally happened on to a young woman working in the capital building in another department who empathized with my predicament. She was also adopted and she understood this driving need I had to know about my family. She managed to acquire a copy of my papers and mail them to me. After that it was fairly easy to trace Janelle's maiden name of Laughlin to her married name of Janelle Josephson."

Marshall tried to imagine what it would be like not knowing the woman who'd given birth to him, not knowing why she'd given him away. The anguish would haunt him, eat at him until he would probably do just as Mia had done. He would search for her and the answers he hungered for.

"That must have been like finding a rainbow in a hurricane," he murmured.

Mia nodded grimly. "Literally. Complete with the pot of gold beneath it. Janelle had come from a very rich family. Her father was a real-estate mogul in and around Denver. They were worth millions and too prominent a part of the community to allow their teenage daughter to raise a child out of wedlock. They tried to pressure her into an abortion but Janelle fought them all the way. Finally they appeared to give in to letting her have the baby, just as long as she would agree to stay with relatives living in another state until I was born."

"Sounds like a pair of real loving parents," Marshall said sarcastically. "She must have been underage and unable to reach out to anyone else for help. So how did they talk her into putting you up for adoption?"

"They didn't. After she gave birth they told her that I'd been stillborn and they didn't want her to go through the trauma of seeing me. They even held a mock funeral to make things look real to Janelle."

"Incredible," he muttered with amazement. "So what happened when she discovered that you were really alive and a grown woman?"

Mia closed her eyes and drew in a ragged breath. "She was shocked, but ecstatic. She immediately took me into her home and began lavishing me with everything, clinging to me as though she couldn't bear for me to get out of her sight."

"What about her husband? What did he think about all this? And her parents—your grandparents—are they still around?"

"Her father died a few years after I was born.

Later on, Janelle's mother became debilitated from a stroke and she now resides in a nursing home. As for her husband, he died a few years ago of a heart attack and since then Janelle has remained a widow."

Frowning now with confusion, Marshall studied her rueful expression. "So you came along and filled Janelle's life up again. That's good. Good for both of you. Wasn't it? *Isn't* it?"

"In many ways, yes. But on the other hand there was Nina—the only mother I'd ever known. It wasn't long before the two women were pushing and pulling me between them. Janelle was offering me a secure home, riches beyond my wildest imaginings. Nina accused me of turning my back on her and ignoring her because she was poor." Her pleading eyes lifted to Marshall's. "That wasn't true, Marshall. But I'm sure it must have seemed that way to Mom."

His hand left hers and lifted to gently touch her cheek. "What was the truth, Mia?"

"The truth?" She let out a mocking laugh. "God, Marshall, I've tried to hide and pretend for so long now I often have to ask myself who I am and what I'm supposed to be doing. But the truth was that I grew to care about Janelle.

How could I not? She loves me and she wants to care for me. Nina loved me, too, but the more I tried to reason with her the more she wanted to drink. She began to cling and whine and tell me that it was all my fault that she couldn't leave the bottle alone. She kept insisting that if I'd come home to her she'd get sober and stay that way."

Marshall's head swung back and forth. "You didn't believe her, did you?"

"Not really," Mia said sadly. "But I didn't want to give up on her completely. I gave her money. Helped her buy a nice home and a car. I thought lifting her out of poverty would help her see that she had every reason to quit drinking. It didn't. She wanted me to come home. One day I agreed to meet with her for lunch—to talk things over and try to reassure her that I would always love her no matter where I lived. I had hopes that I could talk her into entering rehab." She looked away from him and when she spoke again her voice was as hollow as a drained barrel. "She crashed her car on the way to meet me. Later, the toxicology report in the autopsy revealed that she was driving drunk. So now you know. I killed my mother…she died trying to… reach me."

Her chin suddenly dropped to her chest and

silent sobs shook her shoulders. Crushed by the sight of her pain, Marshall moved closer and put his arm around her.

"Mia, don't keep punishing yourself like this. Nina's death wasn't your fault."

Mia lifted her head and stared at him in stunned fascination. "You mean—you don't think I'm a greedy gold digger? That I caused my own mother to kill herself?"

Her questions amazed him. "Is that what you've been afraid of all this time? That if I knew about your past that I wouldn't want anything to do with you? Oh, Mia, can't you see that you didn't cause Nina's death? She was the one who chose to drink. She was the one who climbed behind the wheel."

A sob caught in her throat. "Yes. But I made her unhappy. Because I started making a new life with Janelle."

Groaning, he slipped a hand behind the back of her head and pulled her forward until her cheek was resting against his shoulder. "I've gathered enough from all you've told me that Nina chose to be unhappy long before you found Janelle. She had issues that you weren't qualified to deal with, Mia. She needed professional help. Alcoholism is a horrible disease—you couldn't have cured her just by staying away from Janelle."

Sobbing now with relief, Mia held on to him tightly. "I came here to Thunder Canyon to hide from Janelle. In lots of ways I guess I thought of her as a coconspirator in Nina's death and I resented the love she was trying to give me. I suppose it made me feel even guiltier about Nina. But now I can see that I was wrong about that, too." Lifting her face up to his, she tried to smile. "You've opened my eyes, Marshall. In so many ways."

"I think you should call Janelle. I'm sure she's worried sick about you." He stroked her long black hair with slow, steady movements. "And now that your eyes are open, I hope you can now see that I love you. More than anything, Mia."

She groaned with disbelief. "I don't know why. I'm a bundle of trouble."

"A beautiful bundle," he crooned. He brought his lips over hers in a long, tender kiss. Once it ended, he looked at her pointedly, expectantly. "This means you're going to stay here in Thunder Canyon, doesn't it? With me?"

Slowly, thoughtfully, she eased out of his arms and he watched with a sense of dread as she folded the last of her clothes and placed them in the open suitcase.

"I've got to leave, Marshall. There're so

many unsettled things in my life that I need to deal with right now. It wouldn't be right for me to make promises to you. Not when I need to straighten up my head and my heart." With a tiny flame of hope flickering in her eyes, she glanced at him. "Can you understand that, Marshall? Really understand?"

Rising to his feet, he placed his hands on her shoulders and gave her an affectionate squeeze. "A month ago I probably wouldn't have been able to appreciate what you're feeling. I was so full of myself that I never stopped to really look at my patient's needs or count the blessings that I'd been given. You've changed me, Mia. I'd rather you stay here and not leave my sight." A wry smile touched his lips. "But you've already had enough people pulling and pushing you. I don't want you here with me because you're under duress. If you come back to me I want it to be because you love me, because it's where you want to be."

Turning toward him, she pressed her cheek gratefully against his heart. "Thank you, Marshall, for understanding."

Chapter Fourteen

A week later, in a small cemetery on the outskirts of Alamosa, Colorado, Mia carried bunches of yellow and bronze chrysanthemums as she worked her way to the small patch of ground where her parents lay in rest.

A cool wind was blowing across the graveyard, but a bright sun was shining overhead, glinting off the double granite headstone shared by her parents.

Bending on one knee, Mia brushed away the fallen autumn leaves, then carefully propped the bright cheerful mums against the sparkly black rock. After a moment, she spoke to her mother.

"It's me, Mom. I've come back. Finally. I realize I'm too late to feel your arms wrap around me or to tell you how very much I love you. But I pray that you can somehow hear me now, that you understand I never, ever once stopped loving you.

"After Daddy died we went through so much together. So many hard times. So much sadness. I didn't know how to help you deal with your disease and you didn't know how to fight your way out of it. In the end I guess we were both guilty of not trying hard enough. But I'm positive you've gone on to a better place. And now when I think of you, Mom, I'm going to think of all the good and happy times we had together. I'm going to smile and remember how lucky I was that you chose me to be your daughter."

With a whispered goodbye, Mia rose to her full height and wiped away the single tear on her cheek.

The walk back to her car was short, yet as she lifted her gaze toward the sky, she was certain it had become brighter and there in the vivid blue she could almost envision Nina's smiling face.

Sweet release poured over her like warm sunshine as she pulled a cell phone from her coat pocket and punched in Janelle's number.

Several days later, Marshall was in his office, using the last of his lunch break to make a long distance call to his old friend DJ Traub down in Georgia. For weeks now he'd been trying to talk the other man into coming home once and for all. And today, for the first time, Marshall caught a hint that DJ was seriously considering a return to Montana.

As their conversation reached the end, Marshall made one last pitch to his friend. "All right, buddy, I hope we see you soon. Everybody here misses you. And Thunder Canyon could use some of that good barbecue. There's plenty of space for a Rib Shack here on the resort. Get yourself on a plane and get back here, DJ. No excuses."

Marshall added a quick goodbye and was hanging up the phone when Ruthann paused at the corner of his desk.

"Who was that? I thought I heard you say something about barbecue," she said nosily.

"Sure did. That was DJ Traub. Remember him?"

The nurse thoughtfully tapped a finger against her chin. "I think I do. He's Dax's brother, isn't he?"

"You're right."

"And isn't he the one who made all that money with some sort of barbecue sauce?"

Marshall smiled. "Give the woman a prize. Right on both counts. Besides the sauce he now has a chain of restaurants called DJ's Rib Shack. I'm trying to talk him into putting one here on the resort."

"Oh, now that would be my style of eating," Ruthann told him. "Elbows on the table, paper towels for napkins. The next time you talk to him, tell him he's got one waiting customer for sure."

"I'll be happy to." Marshall reached around to his hip and pulled out his billfold. As he pulled out several large bills and tossed them toward his nurse, he said, "There. Go buy yourself a fancy dress. You and I are going to the Gallatin Room tonight. I promised and now I'm following through. And I don't want to hear any arguments from you, Ruthie."

Frowning, she picked up the bills, counted them, then shook her head in dismay. "I'm not about to waste this money. Like I just told you, I'm not fancy. You need to save this—" she waved the money at him "—and take the heiress to the Gallatin Room."

A shadow crossed Marshall's face. "Have

you forgotten, Ruthie? Mia isn't here at the resort anymore."

Her expression was suddenly apologetic as she sunk into one of the chairs in front of Marshall's desk. "I'm sorry, Marshall. I guess I got so used to you talking about the woman that I forgot she isn't here anymore. Have you heard from her since she left?"

Picking up a pen, he doodled senselessly on a prescription pad. "No. Not yet. But I will. At least, I'm praying that I will."

The nurse studied his glum face. "You got it bad for her, huh?"

He drew in a long breath and released it. For days now, he'd been trying to convince himself that Mia loved him, that one of these days he would look up and see her smiling face. But as each day slipped by without her, he was beginning to worry that she had moved on to a life without him.

"I love her very much, Ruthie. She's changed me. Now I can see that life isn't just a game to be enjoyed. It's a precious gift."

Her expression perceptive, Ruthann leaned forward and touched his hand. "I can see the change in you, Marshall. I'd almost bet that when the snow comes this winter you'll be spending more time here in your office than out on the slopes."

A sheepish smile crossed his face. "I guess I did do a lot of playing last year. It annoyed the hell out of me when I'd have to come in and tend to a patient. I was a real dedicated doctor," he said with sarcasm, then shook his head with a hefty measure of self-disgust. "You know, Ruthie, when the Queen of Hearts struck it rich and the town started going crazy making money, I thought it was the best thing that could have ever happened to this place. I still do think it's helped many people, but it wasn't the right thing for me. I got this cushy job and forgot why I'd become a doctor in the first place."

Ruthann tossed him a look that said she'd watched the circle he'd made and she couldn't be happier that he was back to treating his patients with real care and concern.

"Even if the heiress never comes back, she's been good for you, Marshall. You're back to being a doctor I'm proud to work for."

He wasn't going to even contemplate the idea that Mia would never come back. She had to. She'd become everything to him. "Oh, hell, Ruthie, you're getting maudlin on me now. Get out of here. Go buy that dress. I'm picking you up at seven. So be ready."

The nurse started to toss the money at him, but he grabbed her hand and folded it over the wad of bills.

"Don't argue, Ruthie," he said firmly. "Just do as I say."

"But, Marshall—"

A knock on the office door caused both doctor and nurse to pause and exchange a look of surprise.

"A patient probably took a wrong turn and can't find the exit out of here," Ruthie finally said. "I'll go see."

While Ruthann went to the door, Marshall closed the last chart he'd been updating and flipped off the lamp on his desk.

Rising from the chair, he glanced over to see his nurse was still speaking to someone on the other side of the door. It never failed that a patient would show up when the clinic was closing, but Marshall no longer minded being detained. Not if he could truly help someone.

"There's no need to dawdle around, Ruthie. If someone is sick or injured take the person back to an examining room. I'll be right there."

Ruthann tossed over her shoulder, "This is a patient I'm certain you'll want to see. I'll put her in examining room one."

"Fine. I'll be right there."

Picking up his stethoscope, he hung it around his neck and quickly strode out of his office. When he started down the hallway toward the examination rooms, Ruthann was nowhere in sight. Figuring she'd stayed with the patient, he rapped lightly on the first door he came to and stepped inside.

The moment he spotted Mia sitting on the end of the examining table, he stopped in his tracks and simply stared at her.

Smiling broadly, she said, "I hope you can fix me, doc. I'm really hurting."

"Mia!"

Her name was all he could manage to get out as he rushed forward and enfolded her in his arms.

Mia held him tightly and as the warmth of his body seeped into hers, she knew without a doubt that she had finally come home.

"There's no other place I could be. Except here with you."

Thrilled by her words, he eased his head back far enough to search her smiling face. "You look happy, Mia. Really happy. Are you?"

Her hand lifted to his face and he turned his lips into her palm and pressed a kiss on the soft skin.

"Thanks to you, Marshall. If you hadn't made me face my past I think I would still be running, hiding, trying to forget all the mistakes I have made. Facing them has been more therapeutic than you could ever imagine. Or maybe you can," she added, her eyes twinkling. "You're a doctor. A very special one, too."

He rubbed his cheek next to hers and she closed her eyes and savored the sense of contentment sweeping through her.

"What about your mother—Janelle? I hope you're getting things settled with her."

"Very much so. I think she finally understands that she doesn't have to make demands or smother me to have my love. I've assured her that I'll see her on a regular basis and she can contact me anytime on the phone."

"If you'll answer it, that is," he said wryly.

Her blush was compounded with a guilty smile. "I confess. I had reached the point where I couldn't deal with her, Marshall. But then I met you and fell in love and everything started changing. When I finally saw that you could actually love me for the person I really was— that gave me the courage and strength to face my problems. *You* did all that for me."

His hands cradled the sides of her face as his gaze delved deeply into hers. "Did I hear right? You—fell in love with me?"

The shy smile on her face turned seductive and with a groan of desire, she rested her forehead against his. "I tried hard not to. But you're irresistible, Dr. Cates. Now you're stuck with me. I'm making my home here in Thunder Canyon. And I'm going back to school to finish my nursing studies—especially in counseling. Eventually, I'd like to use my inheritance to create The Nina Hanover Center, a place where women experiencing grief and emotional problems can come to get the help they need. What do you think about that?"

Smiling broadly, he closed the last small space between their lips. "I think it's the grandest thing I've heard since gold was found in the Queen of Hearts. And I just happen to know a good doctor with plenty of strings to help you. We'll build that center together, honey."

Mia's heart sang as she curled her arms around his neck and met the sweet promise of his kiss.

When he finally lifted his head, he shouted with sheer joy and plucked her down from the examining table. "C'mon! Let's go find Ruthie. I promised to take her to dinner tonight at the Gallatin Room. I've got to tell her it's going to be a threesome now." He tugged her toward the door, but before he jerked it open, he snapped his fingers with afterthought. "Hell, let's make it more than a threesome! I'm going to call my family and friends. We'll make tonight a big celebration."

Laughing, Mia followed him down the hallway and knew in her heart that life with Marshall would always be a celebration.

* * * * *

Next month, don't miss
HER BEST MAN
by reader favorite Crystal Green,
the third book in the new
Special Edition continuity
MONTANA MAVERICKS: STRIKING IT RICH

Years ago, DJ Traub left home
to escape a broken heart.
Now he's back and he's got a second chance
with the woman he's never stopped
wanting...

On sale September 2007
wherever Silhouette books are sold.

Welcome to cowboy country...

*Turn the page for a sneak preview of
TEXAS BABY
by Kathleen O'Brien
An exciting new title from
Harlequin Superromance for everyone
who loves stories about the West.*

*Harlequin Superromance—
Where life and love weave together
in emotional and unforgettable ways.*

CHAPTER ONE

CHASE TRANSFERRED his gaze to the road and identified a foreign spot on the horizon. A car. Almost half a mile away, where the straight, tree-lined drive met the public road. He could tell it was coming too fast, but judging the speed of a vehicle moving straight toward you was tricky.

It wasn't until it was about two hundred yards away that he realized the driver must be drunk…or crazy. Or both.

The guy was going maybe sixty. On a private drive, out here in ranch country, where kids or horses or tractors or stupid chickens might come darting out any minute, that was criminal.

Chase straightened from his comfortable slouch and waved his hands.

"Slow down, you fool," he called out. He took the porch steps quickly and began walking fast down the driveway.

The car veered oddly, from one lane to another, then up onto the slight rise of the thick green spring grass. It just barely missed the fence.

"Slow down, damn it!"

He couldn't see the driver, and he didn't recognize this automobile. It was small and old, and couldn't have cost much even when it was new. It was probably white, but now it needed either a wash or a new paint job or both.

"Damn it, what's wrong with you?"

At the last minute, he had to jump away, because the idiot behind the wheel clearly wasn't going to turn to avoid a collision. He couldn't believe it. The car kept coming, finally slowing a little, but it was too late.

Still going about thirty miles an hour, it slammed into the large, white-brick pillar that marked the front boundaries of the house. The pillar wasn't going to give an inch, so the car had to. The front end folded up like a paper fan.

It seemed to take forever for the car to settle, as if the trauma happened in slow motion, reverberating from the front to the back of the car in ripples of destruction. The front windshield suddenly seemed to ice over with lethal bits of glassy frost. Then the side windows exploded.

The front driver's door wrenched open, as if the car wanted to expel its contents. Metal buckled hideously. Small pieces, like hubcaps and mirrors, skipped and ricocheted insanely across the oyster-shell driveway.

Finally, everything was still. Into the silence, a plume of steam shot up like a geyser, smelling of rust and heat. Its snake-like hiss almost smothered the low, agonized moan of the driver.

Chase's anger had disappeared. He didn't feel anything but a dull sense of disbelief. Things like this didn't happen in real life. Not in his life. Maybe the sun had actually put him to sleep….

But he was already kneeling beside the car. The driver was a woman. The frosty glass-ice of the windshield was dotted with small flecks of blood. She must have hit it with her head, because just below her hairline a red liquid was seeping out. He touched it. He tried to wipe it away before it reached her eyebrow, though, of course that made no sense at all. Her eyes were shut.

Was she conscious? Did he dare move her? Her dress was covered in glass, and the metal of the car was sticking out lethally in all the wrong places.

Then he remembered, with an intense relief, that every good medical man in the county was here, just behind the house, drinking his champagne. He found his phone and paged Trent.

The woman moaned again.

Alive, then. Thank God for that.

He saw Trent coming toward him, starting out at a lope, but quickly switching to a full run.

"Get Dr. Marchant," Chase called. "Don't bother with 911."

Trent didn't take long to assess the situation. A fraction of a second, and he began pulling out his cell phone and running toward the house.

The yelling seemed to have roused the woman. She opened her eyes. They were blue and clouded with pain and confusion.

"Chase," she said.

His breath stalled. His head pulled back. "What?"

Her only answer was another moan, and he wondered if he had imagined the word. He reached around her and put his arm behind her shoulders. She was tiny. Probably petite by nature, but surely way too thin. He could feel her shoulder blades pushing against her skin, as fragile as the wishbone in a turkey.

She seemed to have passed out, so he put his other arm under her knees and lifted her out. He tried to avoid the jagged metal, but her skirt caught on a piece and the tearing sound seemed to wake her again.

"No," she said. "Please."

"I'm just trying to help," he said. "It's going to be all right."

She seemed profoundly distressed. She wriggled in his arms, and she was so weak, like a broken bird. It made him feel too big and brutish. And intrusive. As if touching her this way, his bare hands against the warm skin behind her knees, were somehow a transgression.

He wished he could be more delicate. But he smelled gasoline, and he knew it wasn't safe to leave her here.

Finally he heard the sound of voices, as guests began to run around the side of the house, alerted by Trent. Dr. Marchant was at the front, racing toward them as if he were forty instead of seventy. Susannah was right behind him, her green dress floating around her trim legs.

"Please," the woman in his arms murmured again. She looked at him, the expression in her blue eyes lost and bewildered. He wondered if she might be on drugs. Hitting her head on the windshield might account for this unfocused, glazed look, but it couldn't explain the crazy driving.

"Please, put me down. Susannah… The wedding…"

Chase's arms tightened instinctively, and he froze in his tracks. She whimpered, and he realized he might be hurting her. "Say that again?"

"The wedding. I have to stop it."

* * * * *

Be sure to look for TEXAS BABY,
available September 11, 2007,
as well as other fantastic Superromance
titles available in September.

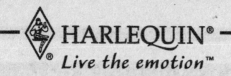

HARLEQUIN®
Live the emotion™

The series you love are now available in

LARGER PRINT!

The books are complete and unabridged—
printed in a larger type size to make it
easier on your eyes.

HARLEQUIN ROMANCE®

From the Heart, For the Heart

HARLEQUIN®
INTRIGUE
Breathtaking Romantic Suspense

HARLEQUIN®
Presents
Seduction and Passion Guaranteed!

HARLEQUIN®
Super Romance®

Exciting, Emotional, Unexpected

Try LARGER PRINT today!

Visit: www.eHarlequin.com
Call: 1-800-873-8635

HLPDIR07

HARLEQUIN ROMANCE®

The rush of falling in love,

Cosmopolitan,
international settings,

Believable, feel-good stories
about today's women

The compelling thrill
of romantic excitement

It could happen to you!

EXPERIENCE
HARLEQUIN ROMANCE!

Available wherever Harlequin Books are sold.

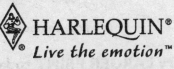

HARLEQUIN®
Live the emotion™

www.eHarlequin.com

HROMDIR04

American ROMANCE®

Invites *you* to experience lively, heartwarming all-American romances

Every month, we bring you four strong, sexy men, and four women who know what they want—and go all out to get it.

From small towns to big cities, experience a sense of adventure, romance and family spirit—the all-American way!

American ROMANCE
Heart, Home & Happiness

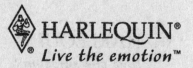

HARLEQUIN®
Live the emotion™

www.eHarlequin.com   HARDIR06

HARLEQUIN®
INTRIGUE®

BREATHTAKING ROMANTIC SUSPENSE

Shared dangers and passions lead to electrifying
romance and heart-stopping suspense!

Every month, you'll meet six new heroes
who are guaranteed to make your spine tingle
and your pulse pound. With them you'll enter
into the exciting world of Harlequin Intrigue—
where your life is on the line
and so is your heart!

THAT'S INTRIGUE—
ROMANTIC SUSPENSE
AT ITS BEST!

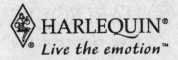

HARLEQUIN®
Live the emotion™

www.eHarlequin.com   INTDIR06

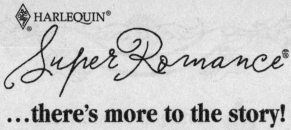

HARLEQUIN®
Super Romance®

...there's more to the story!

Superromance.
A *big* satisfying read about unforgettable
characters. Each month we offer *six* very different
stories that range from family drama to adventure
and mystery, from highly emotional stories to
romantic comedies—and much more! Stories
about people you'll believe in and care about.
Stories too compelling to put down....

Our authors are among today's *best* romance
writers. You'll find familiar names and talented
newcomers. Many of them are award winners—
and you'll see why!

If you want the biggest and best
in romance fiction, you'll get it
from Superromance!

Exciting, Emotional, Unexpected...

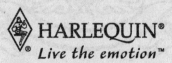

HARLEQUIN®
Live the emotion™

www.eHarlequin.com   HSDIR06

Harlequin® Historical
Historical Romantic Adventure!

*Imagine a time of chivalrous
knights and unconventional ladies,
roguish rakes and impetuous
heiresses, rugged cowboys
and spirited frontierswomen——
these rich and vivid tales will
capture your imagination!*

*Harlequin Historical...
they're too good to miss!*

www.eHarlequin.com   HHDIR06